PRAISE FOR
TUESDAY'S MAH JONGG IS MORE THAN A GAME

"Evocative and insightful, Marsha Temlock's new novel has the effect of bringing her readers to the table of Tuesday's mah jongg game. As we come to know Marlene, Susan, Grace, Barbara, Roseann, and Jennifer, we share the bonds that the game wrought in the players' hearts and minds. A wonderful read!"

—SHARON SOBEL, author of *Madame Cristobel's Secret,*
The Hermitage, and *The Christmas Cameo*

"Marsha Temlock's delightful and funny novel, *Tuesday's Mah Jongg is More Than a Game,* about five women who gather weekly to play the ancient Chinese game of mah jongg and gossip, advise, and care for one another, is a treat to read. The women—Roseanne, Marlene, Susan, Barbara and Grace—all in their late prime, each struggle with life defining issues. Does Roseanne have the strength and energy to care for her grandson, deserted by his parents? Will Marlene continue to repress her own needs while she cares for a dying mother, a narcissistic father, and a husband who calls all the shots? Can the twice-divorced Susan navigate the online dating world at this stage in her life? Can Barbara save her business while dealing with an unfaithful and alcoholic husband? Can Grace, a social worker who cares for everyone, finally take care of herself? As a year passes, we follow each of the women through their crises and dilemmas and cheer for their successes, even as we worry about their missteps and meddling and imperfect solutions. What more can a group of friends wish for but love, support, advice, loyalty, and maybe a good hand each Tuesday at their mah jongg game? By the time I finished the book I wanted to join the ladies at the table and learn to play the game myself."

—FLORENCE REISS KRAUT, author of *How to Make a Life*
and *Street Corner Dreams*

"Marsha Temlock's novel is a story of interlocking female friendships, anchored by their weekly and beloved mah jongg game. Each character has her own distinct flaws, quirks, tribulations, and strengths. The women bicker, meddle, try to solve each other's problems, and rally as one unit when one of the group suffers a catastrophic health event. Most of all, despite their frictions, they love and support one another. Temlock has a gift for making this game come to life on its own—and as a metaphor for the lives of her characters. And mah jongg is a character in its own right. She also has a keen eye for detail. Her descriptions of various surroundings and living spaces are vivid and clever. This novel makes for perfect, stress-free summer reading—perhaps before or after a spirited game of mah jongg. I may just have to learn how to play myself!"

–AMY LOSAK, coauthor, *Wing Strokes Haiku*
and coeditor, *Poised Across the Sky*

TUESDAY'S MAH JONGG IS MORE THAN A GAME

Tuesday's Mah Jongg Is More Than a Game

by Marsha Temlock

© Copyright 2024 Marsha Temlock

ISBN 979-8-88824-391-6

All rights reserved. No part of this publication may be reproduced, stored in a retrieval system, or transmitted in any form or by any means—electronic, mechanical, photocopy, recording, or any other—except for brief quotations in printed reviews, without the prior written permission of the author.

This is a work of fiction. All the characters in this book are fictitious, and any resemblance to actual persons, living or dead, is purely coincidental. The names, incidents, dialogue, and opinions expressed are products of the author's imagination and are not to be construed as real.

Published by

3705 Shore Drive
Virginia Beach, VA 23455
800-435-4811
www.koehlerbooks.com

TUESDAY'S MAH JONGG
IS MORE THAN A GAME

MARSHA TEMLOCK

VIRGINIA BEACH
CAPE CHARLES

Dedicated to my husband, Stephen (1942–2016), and my mother, Jean Sherman. The wind beneath my wings.

CHAPTER ONE

Marlene Corby took down two cut-glass crystal bowls she and Al had gotten forty years earlier as a wedding gift and filled them with assorted nuts and mints. She'd baked an applesauce spice bread that morning and arranged the slices diagonally on a Blue Willow cake plate crazed like a spider's web. The snacks and pitcher of iced tea were on the counter within easy reach of the bridge table covered with a green felt cloth.

Her husband Al, a volunteer firefighter, was attending a special training session. Since he wasn't expected home until six, she'd offered to host the regular Tuesday mah jongg game. Al would want his dinner as soon as he came home. She'd prepared a meatloaf and ratatouille he could heat up in the microwave and bring down to his man cave while he watched the ball game. The sliding door between the kitchen and foyer would muffle any sound should he come home early.

While waiting for the women to arrive, she unloaded the dishwasher and thought about changing her clothes. It was nearly two o'clock and she was still wearing the pilled yellow sweater and saggy jeans from earlier that morning when she'd gone to the supermarket to buy beer to restock the bar refrigerator. The waist was a bit tight and getting tighter around her middle. She was a good cook and probably sampled more than she should. Pretty in a plain, unaffected way, her blunt-cut blond hair was pulled back in a thoughtless ponytail and her porcelain skin was clear and healthy without the help of expensive moisturizers.

She took her mah jongg set off the shelf in the hall closet and spilled the tiles, which clattered onto the bridge table. The tiles were a colorful meld of Chinese characters with different symbols according to suits. The set was Marlene's pride and joy. It was her mother's, a vintage Cardinal 1950s set. The 152 tiles were ivory, and the five racks were made of different colored Bakelite. A set like hers could cost as much as $350 on eBay. The newer sets had racks with attached pushers to make it easy to move the walls of tiles forward, and the tiles came in confectionery colors like pink and lime green. The Chinese characters on the newer sets were easier to read than on her mother's set. The one Bam in her set could be mistaken for a Flower if a player didn't pay attention. But her mah jongg set came with a host of memories of her mother and her friends sitting around the bridge table in the house where she grew up, gossiping and puffing on their cigarettes.

Marlene had learned the complicated rules of the game watching her mother's friends discard the suits of tiles called Bams, Craks, Dots, and Winds (North, East, South, or West). There were also Red, Green, and White (also called Soap) Dragons that matched a particular suit, as well as Flowers, and the prized Jokers that could act in place of any tile.

She had learned how to read the card to complete a particular pattern or hand for mah jongg. The pattern was a kind of cryptogram code categorized by different combinations of letters, numbers, and colors. Hands could comprise evens, odds, consecutive runs, like numbers, singles, pairs, etc. The possible hands were displayed on the mah jongg card. Each year, the National Mah Jongg League (NMJL) created the official card.

The game required skill, strategy, and luck. It could be frustrating if a player did not get the tiles needed to complete a hand. Marlene thought some players took the game far too seriously. She believed the purpose of her weekly game was to have fun. She didn't take losing too seriously and was forgiving if a player made a mistake.

Naturally, there was the anticipation of getting good matching tiles while the tiles were distributed and then planning the hand you wanted to complete. As the play progressed, the mood around the table could be somber while each player concentrated on where the tiles fit in a hand. Marlene liked the euphoria from a winner as much as the groans from a player who was "one away," and the recounting of the failed hands.

Marlene had gotten the original group together. Roseann Pizarro and Barbara Heinz were in her book club. When she suggested they take up mah jongg (the adult education program at the local high school was offering classes), they were excited to learn the game. Susan Gregory was in their class and eager to join the three. They decided to meet on Tuesdays. Susan had recently divorced her husband and was delighted to have a place where she could air her gripes about her ex. It wasn't so much the game that attracted her; it was the companionship of the women.

Although it wasn't strictly legit, Marlene built a two-tier tile wall against each rack before the three women arrived. That way they could begin playing right away. The group had been meeting for almost two years, although there had been some changes when subs were called in if one of the players couldn't make it, like recently, when Roseann had been called away to Florida to take care of her grandson, William. Barbara, a real estate broker, had rented her cottage to Grace, a licensed clinical social worker working toward a private practice. When Barbara told her she played mah jongg on Tuesdays, Grace had expressed interest in learning the game. "It's a way to meet women," she said since she was new to the neighborhood and the game intrigued her. Grace had filled in for Roseann. In a short time, she mastered the mah jongg card and became a whiz at figuring out what someone was playing and switching her hand when her tiles were thrown. But even better, she had a calm, ingratiating manner and the other women loved playing with her.

Grace had become a permanent sub, which meant that after Roseann returned there would be a fourth to fill in if one of the women had a conflict or needed to take a break. In a pinch, there was a way to play three-player mah jongg that had its own rules and variations although the same tiles (fewer of them) and racks were used. This type of mah jongg was played mostly in Japan, Korea, and Malaysia and adapted to suit American play, but the women preferred to play with four and were delighted to have Grace join them.

Marlene checked the time. It was ten minutes to two. The days were getting shorter, the sun hesitant through gray autumn clouds. She tugged the ends of her sleeves while waiting for the women to arrive, hoping the game would begin on time and not run over the two and a half hours they played.

Susan Gregory was the first to arrive. Marlene bolted to the front door when she saw that Susan was parking her Lexus in front of the garage.

"Back up, back up!" she shouted, waving her arms. "You'll be blocking Al when he comes home."

"Oh, shit." Susan reversed her car and backed up a good distance from the garage. Muttering her annoyance, her Chanel tote slung over her shoulder, she stumbled up the unpaved driveway, the heels of her new red Prada boots sinking into the muddy gravel ruts.

Marlene pointed to the doormat. "Do you mind taking off your boots? I just washed the kitchen floor."

Susan struggled out of her gold puffy jacket and pulled off the boots. The leather on the heels was nicked and slick with mud. She was making her way to the living room when Marlene said, "We're playing in the kitchen in case Al comes home early. That way I can close the door and we won't disturb him."

Susan followed Marlene into the gleaming kitchen. Usually, Marlene's house was an icebox, and she'd forgotten to bring a sweater. But today the kitchen was warm and toasty. *Something smells delicious.* She zeroed in on the cake platter. She was famished, having decided to forgo lunch for a manicure after yoga class.

She crinkled her pert ski-jump nose. "Is that banana bread?"

"Apple-spice. Help yourself. We had a bumper crop of apples this year. All week I've been making apple chutney, applesauce, and loaves of apple-spice bread to freeze. Remind me—I've got a bag of apples you can take home."

Susan placed a slice on a paper plate and nibbled a corner of the delicious bread. "Yum. This is worth the extra calories. I'm back on Weight Watchers."

Marlene couldn't fathom why Susan needed to go on a diet. She was rail thin, with small breasts and a child-size waist. The woman never ate anything substantial. The refrigerator in her condo was stocked with diet soda, yogurt, cottage cheese, and rabbit food.

"There's unsweetened iced tea. Help yourself."

"If it's not too much trouble, Marl, I could go for a cup of coffee with low-fat milk, if you have any."

Marlene opened the cabinet over the sink and took down one of Al's souvenir baseball mugs. He'd been collecting mugs and hats ever since she'd known him, and they'd been married forty years. She put a pod in the drip coffee pot. "Barbara and Grace might be a little late. Grace had a last-minute call from a client."

Susan wasn't listening. She was checking her mobile. She had two bars left and was hoping that would be enough if the man she had met online wanted to see her again. They'd gone out for drinks and, while it wasn't exactly a home run, she'd be insulted if he was the one to break it off.

Sighing, she reached for another slice of apple-spice bread. "This really is delicious."

Marlene handed Susan the Dodgers mug. "Sorry, we only have sugar." Susan took a packet of Sweet'N Low from her tote and spilled it into the mug.

"I wish Barbara and Grace would get here. It's getting late." Marlene wanted to avoid Al walking in while they were still playing. Al had said something about having to learn how to use some new computerized system the fire department was using to generate reports.

Last night he'd grumbled, "This computerized stuff is supposed to make things easier for the department, but I think it just makes more work. And it's costing the town a bloody fortune."

Marlene hoped the guys would go out for a beer afterward, which would give her more time to play.

Susan yawned. "God, I'm exhausted. I didn't get home until one last night. I met this guy Martin for drinks to see if there was any chemistry. He turned out to be such a b-o-r-e, but I agreed to see him for dinner tonight, and we talked on the phone for an hour when I got home."

"If he was such a bore when you met for drinks, why did you agree to go out with him for dinner? And why talk on the phone later? What could you have to say?"

"Well, I mean, you never know."

"You never know what?"

"You never know if there's more to the guy."

"Like a criminal record?"

"Oh, please!" Susan pouted. She should have known Marlene would give her the usual heat about how dangerous online dating was. Marlene, who was safely married, even if it was to a male chauvinist, didn't understand what it was like, at her age, to compete with younger women. Divorced twice, Susan knew she didn't have a good record with men. Problem was, she liked men and they liked her—until they didn't.

"Besides, it's not like Martin was a complete bore. He got a lot more interesting as the night wore on." Susan smiled demurely.

"You didn't sleep with him, did you?"

"Oh, really, Marl." Susan picked the tip of her freshly manicured thumbnail. She decided it was best to change the subject. "Any news from Roseann? I've left a dozen messages since we spoke when she first arrived, but now she never returns my calls."

"I think she's just so busy with her grandson, she doesn't have time to make or answer calls." Marlene was a little disappointed she hadn't heard from Roseann, who was her best friend. They used to speak every day and she missed those chitchats.

"Any idea how long she'll be there?" Susan was sitting on a stool. She arched her back, feeling the aftereffects of that advanced yoga class.

"Well, Roseann originally said she'd be back in two weeks, but I think it all depends how long Cindy, that daughter-in-law, stays away.

Roseann rushed down there when Eric called her and said he needed help with the boy. She was rather vague about the situation, just that it sounded like an emergency. Fortunately, she has that house her mother left her in Fort Lauderdale, so the boy can stay with her, although it's only a one-bedroom."

"Well, when you talk to her, tell her we miss her. It was a good thing Grace could sub so we didn't have to break up the game." Susan looked longingly at the sweets Marlene had laid out on the counter.

"Grace said she would reschedule her clients so she could play with us on Tuesdays unless, of course, there's an emergency. She is a really good player and I think she's just about memorized the card."

Susan sighed. "I wish I had a memory like that. With me, one thing flies in, another thing flies out." Just then her cell phone rang. Susan jumped off the stool and went into the living room to take the call. When she returned, she was grinning ear to ear.

"The boring date?" Marlene raised an eyebrow.

"No, another guy I've been chatting with who sounds terrific.

Marlene heard a car moving up the driveway. She got up. "That must be Grace and Barbara. I better warn them to move their car if they park in Al's spot."

Susan took a seat at the bridge table, unfolded her mah jongg card, searched through her tote and took out her Louis Vuitton pouch where she kept the nickels and dimes for paying out the winners, and perched a pair of tortoiseshell reading glasses on her nose. She studied the card to review the odd and even sequences even though she must have played that card fifty times.

A chill whisked though the hallway while Barbara stood in the doorway waiting for Grace who stood outside admiring the beautiful white colonial house. The tip of Barbara's sharp nose was red, her cheeks burnished from the cold. There were dark circles under her brown eyes and deep creases around her mouth.

"Hurry up, Grace. It's friggin' cold," Barbara barked.

"Sorry, it's just so pretty here. All those evergreen trees, and the border of what . . . azaleas?" She shifted her eyes to the large vegetable garden off to the side, now a cemetery of skeleton tomato plants, scrawny cucumber vines, and rotten pumpkins, squash, and eggplants that never made it to harvest.

Barbara unbuttoned her navy-blue jacket and thrust her gloves in her pockets. She unzipped her boots, placing them next to Susan's red ones on the mat. When Grace came in, she stepped out of her thrift-store UGGs and removed a wide hand-knitted woolen shawl she'd draped over an embroidered tunic in sunset colors that flattered her bronze complexion, rouged cheeks, and cherry-red lipstick. She was a tall woman in her midforties with straight shoulder-length coal-black hair tucked behind small earlobes pierced with large silver hoops.

"Here, let me take your coats," Marlene said.

"I was admiring your garden. It must be wonderful to have all those homegrown vegetables," Grace said.

"Oh, it is. I love gardening. It's relaxing but also frustrating," she admitted, "competing with the rabbits and deer. Al built the fence, and it helps but doesn't seem to discourage the squirrels and a certain woodchuck."

Grace followed Marlene into the kitchen where Susan was searching for an outlet to charge her phone.

"I hope I didn't keep you waiting," Grace said. "I had to take a call from a client who was freaking out at his job site. Nice guy and all, but he needs a lot of support. I have been *sooo* looking forward to this afternoon. You'd never believe my morning. It must be the phases of the moon." She sniffed. "Don't tell me you baked!"

"Apple-spice bread."

"My favorite. Oh, I almost forgot." She reached into her canvas carryall. "I brought you those jellies you liked so much."

"Why, thank you, Grace. If you like the bread, I'll give you the recipe. And there's a bag of apples you can take back with you. We have enough apples for the entire neighborhood."

"I'd love that. Oh good, you built the walls." Grace sat down and placed her mah jongg card in front of an orange rack and positioned her long, tapered fingers at the edge of the table, ready to begin the play.

Barbara took the chair between Grace and Susan. "You're East, Marlene, since it's your house. Technically, you should have waited for us to build our own walls," she said stiffly, and moved Susan's cell to make room for her gray quilted money pouch.

"Sorry. I thought we could save time, but if it really bothers you, Barbara, we can knock them down and rebuild them."

"That won't be necessary." Susan frowned at Barbara. "I doubt Marlene arranged the tiles so she'd get all the Jokers."

It was easy to see that Barbara was in a foul mood. She wanted to explain that Hank had had a bad night, that he tossed and turned and kept her awake. She'd hardly gotten any sleep, and she felt a migraine coming on. But she was a private person, and she did not want to share her latest marital problem with the group. Although this was a place where the women usually took comfort knowing they were among friends and that whatever was said here, stayed here.

"Your house, Marlene, you're East," Barbara reminded Marlene again since Marlene seemed somewhat distracted. The fact was, Marlene couldn't help worrying that Al might come home early and interrupt the game, even though she had confirmed with him before he left that the training would last until six, and the game should be over by then. But they were starting a bit late today.

I should have called him to see how the training session was going, she thought, *but then Al would be annoyed if I interrupted whatever he was doing.* She knew the only reason to call Al when he was at the firehouse was if there was some kind of home emergency. Obviously, hosting her mah jongg ladies did not fall into that category.

"Do you want to throw the die for a hot row?" Grace asked.

"No. I hate that hot row," Marlene said. "I think it limits our chances of winning since we can't call a tile unless it's for mah jongg."

Barbara raised her eyebrows. She was frustrated with the women. Although there were certain conventions about how to play mah jongg—every game had its own rules, and some games were stricter than others—she dearly wished this group would settle the dispute of the hot wall. She said heatedly, "Well, I disagree. A hot row makes the game more challenging." At which point, she began lining up her tiles on her rack.

"I thought you were supposed to wait until all thirteen tiles have been distributed before putting them on your rack. Isn't that one of the rules we decided on?" Susan smirked, one more time checking her mobile. She so enjoyed putting Barbara in her place. Barbara could be such a stickler.

Marlene frowned. "Susan, whatever has gotten into you?"

Susan shrugged. "Sorry. Maybe I shouldn't have skipped lunch."

As hostess, Marlene didn't like the way the game was starting off; there was too much tension in the air. She dealt the remaining tiles, hoping things would improve. No one said anything while they arranged the thirteen tiles on their racks. Because she was East, Marlene got one more tile and would be the first one to discard a tile. During the Charleston, they passed tiles they did not want to complete a possible pattern they had chosen. The Charleston consisted of passing three tiles to the right, across, and to the left in a regulated sequence until the optional passing, after which play could begin. This all was prescribed by the NMJL.

When they were ready to start the game, Marlene discarded a two Dot. Susan discarded a North, Barbara a two Dot, and Grace a five Bam. The kitchen was quiet as a tomb once play proceeded except for the moans, groans, and usual complaints: "I have shit," "Why in bejesus's name did I do that," "I could use four Jokers," "Someone is holding my tiles," blah, blah, blah.

The tiles clattered and splattered on the felt cloth until the jubilant announcement: Mah jongg! Gleefully, Barbara collected three quarters and put them in her pouch.

They began the next game, turning and scrambling the tiles facedown, and building new two-tier walls against their racks.

The game proved to be a source of strength for the women who, through the years, had created a bond that was more than just a social connection. Blessedly, theirs was a friendly game. Marlene recounted how she was once invited to play in a game where one woman accused another of cheating. "All hell broke loose, and the women were at each other's throats. Another time, one of the women criticized me for helping a newcomer who was about to make a mistake."

"I would never play with that kind of women," Susan said with a snort.

Grace was quick to point out that mah jongg was their opportunity to forget their problems and, for heaven's sake, have fun.

"In a way it's kind of group therapy," Susan commented. "And a lot cheaper than my shrink."

"You could say that." Grace turned to Barbara and wondered if the game was helping her relax. She tended to take the game more seriously than the others and was staring daggers at Susan, who had been successful in charging her phone and was now checking her messages.

"Your turn, Susan," Barbara snapped.

"Oh, shit," Susan wailed, counting fourteen tiles. "I think I'm dead."

"You needed to discard a tile after taking my Joker when you replaced my white Dragon," Marlene pointed out.

"I did, but I don't know what to throw!"

"Throw something that's already out," Grace suggested, trying to defuse the mounting tension.

Barbara screwed her lips. She was one away from mah jongg and counting on a two Dot to complete her hand. "If you'd put that goddamn phone away and concentrate on the play maybe you'd know what to do."

"Okay, okay. Give me a minute. I'm thinking."

"Well, do a little less thinking and just throw a tile," Barbara commanded. Her head was splitting, and she was disgusted with the slow pace of the play.

"You sound like you should be playing in that game Marlene told us about," Susan shot back.

Marlene looked at her watch. It was five fifteen. She too wished the pace of the game would pick up.

Susan drummed her fingers. "Flower."

Barbara's voice rose to a fevered pitch. "Flower? Don't you see what Grace laid out?"

Susan looked blankly at the tiles exposed on Grace's rack. "Well, she could be playing any number of hands," she retorted.

"Obviously, she's playing a hand that needs Flowers, and you just discarded a Flower, which could have given her mah jongg."

"But it didn't give her mah jongg."

Exasperation welled in Barbara. "I just wish you'd take some time to study the card the way you do your dating sites."

Susan harrumphed and deliberately looked at her cell to further annoy Barbara.

"Now ladies, it might be a good idea if we didn't use our phones while we're playing," Grace suggested, "unless there is some emergency—I know I have clients calling me all hours of the day—in which case we can set them to vibrate."

"Well, I for one don't consider Susan's dating sites an emergency." Barbara glowered at Susan.

"I agree," Marlene said, equally annoyed with Susan's behavior. "Let's do what Grace suggested."

The game proceeded without further comment. Gradually the air cleared while the women played out their hands. It looked like it was going to be a wall game when Barbara sang out, "Mah jongg, and it's a concealed hand. That will cost you double." Triumphant, she exposed her completed pattern on top of her rack. "That's fifty cents from each of you." She zipped her winnings into her pouch and tossed the winning hand onto the table with the other tiles, eager to begin the next game when the garage door groaned.

Marlene leaped to her feet, nearly knocking over her glass of iced tea. She caught her breath. The kitchen door slid open, and Al stepped in the kitchen.

Al was a big man, tall and burly with wide shoulders and a thick neck. With a massive nest of gray hair and a grisly beard, he was a formidable figure, especially towering over the bridge table that seemed to shrink in size with his approach.

Marlene ran up to him. She was five foot three and barely reached his shoulders, but she wrapped her arms around his middle. "You're home early." Al freed himself and looked past his wife. "I didn't realize you were having the game."

"But I told you, and you weren't due home until six. We were just finishing up. I'm afraid the game is running a little late," she apologized, not looking at the women who had turned into statues. "Why don't you take a shower and change while we finish up here? You must be exhausted. I bought you some beer. It's in the downstairs refrigerator and I made your dinner. There's meatloaf and ratatouille I'll heat up. I made the ratatouille the way you like it—not too tomatoey. I'll bring your plate down to you when you've showered and changed," she told him, hoping to give the women time to leave before Al came back downstairs.

Marlene's anxiety was palpable. It was like a tidal wave swept the women into action. On cue, the three began putting the tiles every which way in the compartments in the mah jongg case.

Sensing the discomfort of the women, Grace turned to Al and said with a smile in her voice, the one she used to calm down clients, "Marlene mentioned you are a volunteer fireman. I've worked with some local departments. I get called in to counsel the team if one of the men is hurt or, sadly, dies. You show a lot of courage to put yourself at risk like that."

Al puffed up a bit. "We do more than just respond to fire alerts. Sometimes it's helping out in the community. Today, for example, I got a call from the Meadows Nursing Home. One of the old ladies locked herself in the bathroom and wouldn't open the door. We couldn't jimmy the lock, so I had to break a window to get to her. She was screaming that she couldn't breathe. I thought she might be having a heart attack. I had to carry her down the ladder and I swear she must've weighed two hundred and fifty pounds."

"Is she okay?" Marlene asked, fixing her eyes on the tiles being put upside down and right side up in the mah jongg case. She preferred the double-layered tiles be stacked with the embossed side down. That was what her mother had taught her years ago, when she'd presented Marlene with her treasured set. "You'll want to protect the etched designs," she'd explained, "from knocking into each other." But Marlene was too anxious to correct the women.

Al was saying, "Yeah. But crazy as a loon. Kept calling me Luke."

"You probably reminded her of her son or husband," suggested Grace.

Marlene could no longer contain her annoyance. She angled herself to face the women. "Never mind about cleaning up, ladies. I'll put the rest away. Hon, why don't you go upstairs and take that shower, so you don't miss the game."

Al's footfalls could be heard above them while Marlene stood in the hallway sorting coats. "I'm sorry we had to break up the game early."

"Oh, it's all right," Grace assured her. "Thanks for hosting and for baking the apple-spice bread."

"Yes, thanks for everything, Marl. Where are we playing next week?" Susan clicked the calendar app on her cell.

"I think it is my turn and I would have you at my place . . . but . . ." Barbara stumbled, hesitant to explain that Hank was out of sorts, and she dare not trust his moods now that he was spending more time at home. Susan came to the rescue. "I would be more than happy to be next week's host. How about I order sandwiches so we could have lunch and begin a bit earlier? My treat."

"That would be lovely, but you have to let us chip in," Grace said.

"That won't be necessary, Grace. I can handle it."

Barbara buttoned her coat and searched for her car fob. "Come on, Grace."

"Wait everyone, I want to give you a bag of apples," Marlene called out. "Come this way. I have a bag for each of you. And I'll send you the recipe. Your name is on your bag."

The three women followed Marlene to the back porch and picked up their bag of apples. Susan had no idea what she was going to do with her apples when she got home. Certainly not bake an apple-spice bread.

Late autumn smelled of leaf mold and wood ash. A breeze whipped up and Marlene had to hold the screen door open so it wouldn't fly back in their faces. The stairs leading down to the backyard were steep and slick with fallen leaves from the previous night's rainfall. A quarter to six and it was almost dark.

"Damn, the porch light is out. Be careful going down the stairs and mind the flowerpots," Marlene warned. She could hear the television in the man cave and knew Al had gotten himself a beer and was listening to the game, which would hopefully put him in a better mood.

Feeling their way in the semidarkness, the women clung to the handrail and slowly made their way down the stairs to the backyard. The moon was ringed in mist.

"Fuck," Susan cried out, almost losing her footing and clutching the air. "Fuck, fuck. My heel caught on a nail or something. Now my boots really are ruined."

Marlene groaned. "I'm so sorry. I told Al to fix that step. I guess he was too busy and forgot. Good night, ladies. See you next week." She hurried back into the house to heat Al's dinner.

"Hold on to me," Grace cautioned Barbara, who was trying to hold the bag of apples while finding her way to her car.

Susan walked behind, muttering. "Fuck. What a nightmare. I'm glad that's over with. How the hell does she put up with him?"

"She loves him is how," Barbara answered curtly. "When you love someone, you put up with a lot of shit." Didn't Susan know that caring about someone and wanting to please him to satisfy the ravenous hunger inside you meant sacrificing a part of yourself? What she wanted to say, but restrained herself, was, "Maybe that's why your marriages never lasted."

"Good night. See you next week, and remember, I'm having lunch," Susan yelled out the open window, backing up and careening into the border of bushes along the driveway.

Grace settled herself in Barbara's car. The heater blasted warm air, a welcome relief to the chill that ran through her after such a disquieting ending to the mah jongg get-together. "I thought Al was really nice the way he helped that old woman in the nursing home, didn't you?"

"All I heard was Al complaining about how heavy she was. Seems to me anyone who can carry someone who weighs two hundred and fifty pounds down a ladder can carry his own friggin' dinner to his man cave. I need a stiff drink."

Grace laughed. "I think Susan is too critical of Al. I wonder why."

"You know Susan was divorced twice. She's just bitter about men, although she keeps joining those dating sites. If you ask me, she was too quick to get out of her marriage to the last guy—who I thought was really nice. You don't run at the first sign of problems."

Grace studied her friend. She bit her lip but decided to say what she was reading into Barbara's comment about running too soon. "Maybe you're selling Susan short. You don't really know the guy she was married to. No one knows what goes on behind closed doors. I think Susan tried, but in the end, she wasn't willing to sacrifice herself. I felt the same way and that's why I left my marriage. I knew it would be hard for me and the boys, but we would, in the long term, be better off if I was happy. There are some problems you just can't solve in a marriage as much as you try to—if the other person isn't willing, that is."

"And you're suggesting . . . "

"I'm not suggesting anything," Grace protested, realizing she might have touched a sore spot and should be more mindful of what she said to Barbara. "You seem on edge today. Is everything all right?"

"Everything is fine. I've just had some problems at work. Selling real estate is not a walk in the park." Barbara snorted, hoping that lie would satisfy Grace's curiosity about what was really bothering her.

"Grace, I'm sorry I was so short-tempered this afternoon."

"Well, you were a bit hard on Susan."

"I guess."

Barbara's eyes filled with tears. She wanted to tell Grace what was really on her mind. The truth was, she dreaded going home, fearing the worst if Hank was there or if he wasn't and she had to face that too.

Back in her kitchen, Marlene collected Al's dirty dishes and put the refreshments away. She reheated some leftover lamb stew for herself, sat down, and ate her dinner while reading last month's *Bon Appetit*. By the time she was finished cleaning the kitchen and sweeping the floor, the game was over. She went into the hallway to put the mah jongg set away and noticed the mail on the hall table. She had brought it in that morning, after going to the supermarket to buy Al's beer, then forgot about it.

In addition to her subscriptions to cooking magazines and the home decorating catalogs where she looked for ideas for sprucing up the house, there were two letters for Al. She did not recognize the name of the company—Howland and Brighton, Bridgeport, Connecticut. Funny, but there had been two others from the same company last week and a couple the week before that. They must be invoices, she decided. Invoices for what? She didn't recall buying anything from Howland and Brighton and made a mental note to ask Al tomorrow. Maybe the letters had something to do with their insurance policies; he'd been grumbling about the rates and talking about changing companies. That must be it. Her mind was taken up with her mother, whose health was failing, so she didn't pay attention to that stuff and let Al handle it. She'd call her mother tomorrow since she couldn't face any more upset. She was also worried about Roseann, who had left that day for Florida. She sighed. There was some problem with Eric who said he needed her to take care of the boy. Marlene didn't know what the problem was. Roseann didn't offer an explanation. She just said it was an emergency and it couldn't wait. She paid full fare for her ticket. Poor Roseann. She sighed again. It wasn't easy having a son like Eric. And then Jack dying a year ago. Now Roseann was all alone, left to sort things out by herself. Marlene didn't envy her friend. Her Al could be a bit of a trial. She was well aware how the women felt about him. He had his faults, but no man was perfect. Nothing in life was perfect, she told herself. You just had to make the best of what you had.

When Al came back upstairs, he saw Marlene sitting at the kitchen counter, her head in her hands. "Sorry, babe, if I broke up your ladies' game."

"That's okay, Al. It was time to stop. It was our last game anyway."

"You coming to bed?"

"I think I'll finish reading my magazine; you go on ahead."

A half hour later she decided it was time to go to bed. She turned off the downstairs lights and headed upstairs. She'd talk to the doctor next week when she took her mother for her appointment, praying the news wasn't as bad as she thought.

Al was in bed, snoring. She didn't mind that he was asleep and had not waited up. The fact that he was there, that she had married someone she could rely on, someone who cared about her as deeply as she cared for him, that was all that mattered. She tucked her feet under his and drifted off.

CHAPTER TWO

The weather in South Florida was cooler than Roseann expected but better than the freezing temperature when the driver had picked her up at six in the morning and taken her to JFK for her flight out. Her flight had been delayed an hour. By the time the plane landed, she was exhausted, and the day had only just begun.

She paid another visit to the bathroom before she found the car-rental kiosk. She smoothed her brown hair, now graying at the roots, put drops in her hazel eyes, and dabbed the coffee stain on the front of her blouse with a damp paper towel. She felt as dowdy as she looked. What did that matter? She was an invisible sixty-eight-year-old grandmother on a mission.

The young girl at the rental counter looked up from her mobile. "Welcome to Easy Trip Rentals. What kin I do fer ya?"

Roseann rested her tote bag on top of her suitcase. "I reserved a car in the name Roseann Pizarro. P-i-z-a-r-r-o."

"Just a sec . . . yup . . . Crestwood, Connecticut? A compact?"

Roseann breathed a sigh of relief. "That's right."

"May I see your license and credit card? Car insurance is fifteen dollars a day."

"No thank you." She recalled Jack declining the insurance since their own auto policy would cover any damages to the car.

"We'll fill the gas tank when ya bring it back."

They charge more per gallon than at the gas station, Jack had said.

"That won't be necessary," Roseann told her, struggling to remove her license from the plastic pocket in her wallet.

"Sign here." The girl handed her the rental agreement.

Roseann put on her bifocals, signed the agreement, and returned the cards to her wallet. "I'm going to Fort Lauderdale. Do you have a map showing the way to the highway?"

"Ya got the address? Plug it into Waze," the girl said like Roseann was a Luddite who had never used a cell phone or computer.

Granted she wasn't an expert, and Susan had had to show her how to use Uber, but hadn't she made her airline reservation online when she couldn't get through to the airline after Eric had called her? "I find it easier to follow a map," she said.

The young girl disappeared below the counter for a few seconds. The map she unfolded had seen better days. She highlighted the route to the highway and circled two exits to Fort Lauderdale.

Roseann wasn't sure which exit was the one to take. Jack had always done the driving. But Jack was gone, lost to pancreatic cancer. It didn't seem possible, but it would be a year in July.

"Aisle C, Space Eighty-One."

"Excuse me?"

"That's where the car is. It's a blue Camry." She handed Roseann the key fob. "Enjoy your stay."

Roseann picked up the map and the rental packet and put both in a pocket in her carryall. "Thank you, dear. You've been very helpful." She telescoped the handle of her suitcase. Dragging it behind her as she trudged through the parking lot, she repeated, "Aisle C, Space Eighty-One" like a mantra until she located the car.

The car was not that different from the one she drove at home, although this one was a newer model. Because Jack always checked for dents and tested the air conditioner before driving off, she walked around the car taking inventory. It looked fine. She put her suitcase in the trunk and adjusted the driver's seat and mirrors. The controls were like those she was used to, and she felt right at home behind the wheel, but still nervous about getting off at the right exit.

She drove past the billboards she remembered from previous trips: Bud's Eat-All-You-Can Buffet and that huge photograph of three accident lawyers—ambulance chasers with their shit-eating grins, Jack used to say. And her all-time favorite, The Happy Hockers Pawn Shop. She felt a lot better knowing she was heading in the right direction after seeing the billboards.

Eric said he was dropping William off around five. Since it was a little past one, she had enough time to stop at Publix and pick up a few groceries. She had no idea what her grandson liked to eat. What if he had allergies? So many kids today were allergic to just about everything.

To be on the safe side, she would avoid anything with nuts and briefly considered a box of Froot Loops before deciding that too much sugar made kids hyperactive and settling on a package of frozen waffles for tomorrow's breakfast. What about pizza? Kids loved pizza. Next, she stopped by the meat section and looked over the chopped meat. She could make meatballs and spaghetti for tomorrow night's dinner, although it was hard to plan ahead since she had no idea what tomorrow would look like.

Bending over to put the groceries in the backseat of the car, she felt lightheaded and realized she hadn't eaten anything since the pretzels and coffee on the flight—and a good portion of the coffee had ended up on her blouse at that. What she needed was a quick bite to tide her over. But instead of going to the coffee shop in the mall, she stepped into Walgreen's and bought a fifty-piece puzzle, a coloring book and crayons, and a box of dominoes. Rainy day activities when they couldn't go to the beach or the pool. How was she supposed to entertain an eight-year-old until her daughter-in-law picked him up?

And when exactly was Cindy coming? Eric had been so vague. He just said Cindy was in Boulder and that her company was expanding out West. Cindy sold time-shares, so it was possible she was looking into job opportunities that would pay her more than she was currently earning. That was one of the things Roseann liked about Cindy—she was ambitious. What she didn't like was Cindy's superior attitude. She acted like Roseann spent all her time shopping and playing mah jongg. Which was far from the truth.

Roseann had waited until Eric was in middle school before she went back to work. She believed her place was taking care of her family. She volunteered at Eric's middle school and then, when she heard the principal's secretary was leaving, she applied for the job and got it. At her retirement party nearly twenty years later, Mr. Hunt had handed her a bouquet of flowers and said, "Roseann is the glue that holds Jackson Middle School together."

Another thing that worried Roseann was the prospect that Cindy would be moving to Boulder with William now that she and Eric were separated. She was one of her company's top salespeople. The company had a new complex of time-shares in Boulder and wanted her to manage the sales force. Roseann hated to admit it, but unless Eric moved out West and found a job, which she doubted, he would never get to see William. Eric was in no condition to go anywhere until he straightened himself out—and God only knew when that might happen.

Roseann cracked the car window. The balmy breeze was a relief after the cold weather back home. She fanned her flushed cheeks and patted her forehead with a crumpled tissue. She had a lot to do when she got to the villa: make up the sofa bed, set out clean towels, dust the furniture, maybe start cooking those meatballs that always tasted better reheated the next day. *Almost forgot. Better let the condo association know that William will be staying with me for two weeks.* The board was very strict about owners registering their visitors since the break-ins this year.

Roseann drove up to the gatehouse and greeted Max, the security guard.

"Long time, no see, Mrs. Pizarro. Will Mr. Pizarro be joining you?"

"He passed," she murmured, a lump in her throat.

"Oh, I'm very sorry to hear that. Mr. Pizarro was such a nice man." Roseann was sure that Max had outlived many of the original owners at Sundial Acres.

"Thank you, Max. My grandson is staying with me for a couple of weeks. Eric will be dropping him off around five."

"I'll look out for him then. I'm here until six. Again, sorry about your husband. Enjoy your grandson now. Have a nice evening."

"Thank you. You too."

Roseann drove past the high-rise condo whose tiered wrought-iron terraces clung to a pink stucco exterior stained with rust. The next section was the town houses. The units circled a man-made body of water with spouting fountains and palm trees festooned with little lights.

The single-family villa she'd inherited when her mother died was one of dozens of boxy pastel-colored houses, each with a postage-stamp front lawn and rear screened-in lanai. The backs of the houses ran the full length of a narrow canal said to be home to sleepy-eyed alligators and snapping turtles. The idea of the alligators lying in wait had been the bane of her parents' existence when Eric was a little boy who liked to throw rocks into the canal hoping to goad the alligators onto the banks.

Roseann parked her car in the small garage. Instead of going into the house through the garage entrance, she walked up the short path leading to the porch where her parents used to sit and watch the Sundial Acres world go by on bicycles, tricycles, and golf carts. Fuchsia, pink, and orange bougainvillea vined over the porch railing. The aroma was heavenly. She'd forgotten how peaceful it was here, how much she'd enjoyed their family vacations during school breaks. Now with Jack and both her parents gone, the house was more a responsibility than a place to relax. But perhaps she could recapture that feeling spending time here with William. She certainly hoped so.

Roseann used her key to unlock the front door and stood in the small, mirrored hallway, blinking away tears. The house echoed loss. She set her things down in the bedroom and went into the bathroom to pee. She paid Mr. D'Amico to flush the toilets, run the faucets, and adjust the temperature according to the season. He had prepared for her arrival, but the house still smelled a bit musty from being closed up, and Mr. D'Amico had left the shades down to keep the house cooler.

She would air it out by opening the windows and roll up the window shades to let in more light.

When her mother died, rather than selling their house, Roseann threw herself into redecorating. She gave her parents' furniture to Goodwill and bought a rattan living room ensemble. The sleep sofa and two club chairs were upholstered in a green-and-white fern pattern. She filled faux Venetian glass vases with colorful silk flowers, outfitted the dining room with a shimmering glass-and-chrome table and rattan chairs upholstered in the same matching fern fabric as the sofa and club chairs, and hung pictures of sea animals and flamingos on seafoam-painted walls. The only remnants of her parents' furnishings were family photographs and her mother's collection of Hummel figurines she didn't have the heart to give away. Yet.

Her cell phone vibrated. "I swear that woman has radar," Roseann grumbled, looking at the phone number.

"Hello, Roseann?"

"Yes, Marlene."

"Finally. I've been calling since early this morning. Why didn't you pick up?"

"It's been hectic. Sorry."

"How was the flight?"

"Fine, although it was an hour late taking off. I just came back from grocery shopping. Listen, I really have no time to talk. I've a million things to do before Eric drops William off."

"If you had taken a later flight, I would have driven you to the airport."

"I told you that wasn't necessary. I left at six and took an Uber."

"When is Eric coming?"

"Around five."

"Does he know how long he'll be away this time?"

Away. Marlene knew very well that Eric was going into rehab. Why didn't she just come out and say it?

"It's a residential detox program. It depends on how he does.

The good thing is there are outpatient therapy sessions he'll have to attend afterward."

"Which means you might have to watch William for more than two weeks."

"Cindy will be here in two weeks," she said shortly. "Like I said, I really don't have time to talk."

"Where is she?" Marlene persisted.

"Boulder."

"Boulder? What's she doing there?"

"She's there on business."

There was dead silence while Marlene waited for Roseann to fill in the details, which she didn't have. Eric was vague about Cindy, the upcoming divorce, the custody arrangements. He was vague about everything, except he did say that Cindy was considering a transfer to Boulder. Roseann was afraid to press him when he was in this condition.

"William is not going to like being separated from his parents. It won't be easy having him with you."

"Oh, we'll work it out." Roseann removed the throw pillows from the sleep sofa and put them on one of the club chairs. Eric could help her open the couch. "I'm actually looking forward to spending time with William."

"When did you last see him?"

"Eric brought him back for Jack's funeral, but I hardly spent any time with him."

"Eric should have stayed longer to help you tie up the loose ends after Jack died."

Roseann hitched up her shoulders. Marlene was her best friend, but sometimes she exasperated her with her negativity. "There were no loose ends, Marlene. Jack was very organized. He did everything he could to make it easy for me."

She refused to cry every time his name came up. But oh, how she missed Jack. *Jack.* She thought about him every day, although there were times when she could not remember his voice or the color of his eyes. She was more afraid of remembering him wrong than forgetting him entirely. Jack had not been perfect, but he'd been better than she thought she deserved. And now, she owed him this much. To make one last effort to guard what was theirs. William. He was their legacy.

Marlene was saying she was more than willing to come down to be with her if she needed an extra set of hands. "Al's so busy with Rotary. He's heading up a fundraising event for the Lobster Fest this spring. Honestly, it won't be a problem."

"That really won't be necessary, but I appreciate the offer. And you have enough to juggle with your mother. How is she?"

"The same. Stable for now. That's why I thought I could get away for a few days." What Marlene wasn't admitting is that she could use a break from both her mom and Al.

"Thanks for calling. Like I said, I have a lot to do before they arrive."

"Promise me you'll call."

"I promise, Marlene. We'll be fine. Don't worry so much."

Roseann clicked off the phone. She stared into space thinking about her friendship with Marlene. She was blessed to have her and the other women from the mah jongg game in her life, especially when Jack was sick and right after he died, but there were times, like now, that she needed to be alone to adjust to the changes in her life.

She felt very tired all of a sudden. She lay down on the couch, closed her eyes, and was asleep in minutes. She dreamed she was at the beach, carrying a child into the water. A wave swept her and the child under and for a long time there was nothing but stillness. When she surfaced, she was still holding the child until he jumped out of her arms and swam to shore. Roseann managed to get to the shore, calling his name while he ran away from her. He was too fast. She couldn't catch up to him. Breathing hard, her heart thumping in her chest, she stood helpless. William! she screamed. An alligator was at her feet.

Roseann woke up with a start, hugged herself. What was she dreaming? Then it came to her. There were alligators in the canal out back. She'd forgotten all about that. Oh, dear God. She had to make sure that William never went to the canal, but how to stop a boy from playing there? He would want to look for turtles and try fishing. And she couldn't watch him every minute, could she?

She was a bundle of nerves. She needed to keep busy. She would open the sleep sofa herself because it looked like Eric was going to be later than he'd said. William would be tired, so she would give him his dinner right away and then run a bath. He could watch some TV, or she could read him a book. Only, damn, she hadn't bought any. She'd take him to the library; there was a good kids' section.

Roseann heard the truck even though she had gone to the backyard to check on the fruit trees her parents had planted—grapefruit and orange trees that were good producers. Years before, she and her mother had made juice from the ripe fruit.

The truck needed a new muffler, and the exhaust system was shot. Roseann walked quickly down the path and watched Eric park in front of the wrong villa. Kate Timothy was going to have a fit.

Eric got out of the truck. He didn't walk, he strode up to her, shouting, "Hey, Ma!" as if she were a mile away instead of standing on the porch steps just three feet away.

For a second, she didn't recognize him. *He's grown a beard and let his hair grow wild.* Up close she could see his face had a sickly pallor. *He's lost so much weight.* "Eric, I was worried about you." She sounded more alarmed than she meant to. Then anger crept into her tone. "You said you'd be here around five and it's nearly six."

Eric leaned over and pecked her on the cheek. "How's my special lady?" She flinched. He smelled rank, like one of the homeless she always avoided when she went to New York to see a show or go shopping.

"Where's William?" she asked.

"He's in the back seat, playing a video game on his phone."

"Well, for heaven's sake. Go get him."

Eric went back to the truck. He'd lost so much weight his jeans sagged in the rear, lowered around his hips.

She stood there, frowning, while he opened the back door, and heard him yelling. "I told you to get out. NOW!"

Just then, Kate Timothy, her neighbor on the left, came out of her house to get the Sundial Acres newsletter on her doormat. She tucked it under her arm and glowered at the beat-up truck.

"That's my son's," Roseann explained quickly. "He's just stopping by to drop off my grandson, who will be staying with me for a couple of weeks."

"Oh. That's nice. What's his name?"

"William."

"I thought he was Eric."

"William is my grandson. Eric is my son."

"How long did you say he's staying?" Kate listed to the left and cupped her ear.

"Just a couple of weeks while his parents are on vacation," she lied.

"I hope you'll be available for mah jongg while you're here, Roseann. We could always use a fifth."

"I'm afraid not, Kate. But thanks for asking. I'll be too busy with *William*," she said raising her voice.

"Was it very cold when you left? I heard they were expecting a big snowstorm up North."

"Not that I know of."

She looked at the truck and saw that Eric had disappeared into the back seat. There was more commotion. Roseann shuddered, thinking the worst.

Kate angled her head toward the street. She shouted, "There seems to be a problem with your grandson," and pointed to the truck.

"I think the child was sleeping and his father is trying to get him up."

"I'm glad you're back, Roseann. Stop by and see me."

"I better go see to my son and grandson."

"Your dear mother and father, may they both rest in peace, loved it here."

Thankfully, Roseann was saved by the sprinklers. A rainbow

pulsated over the two lawns and Kate retreated into her house, the *Sundial Acres News* tenting her head.

Roseann headed toward the truck, hesitated, chewed her bottom lip. She planted her feet on the path and stood there, a few feet from the truck. *Should I go up to the child?* Her instinct told her to stay back.

Finally, Eric emerged with his arm around William's shoulder, dragging him toward her.

William was howling like a small animal caught in a trap. "I don't want to go."

She gazed at him and said as gently as she could, "Hello, William. I'm so glad you're here. Boy, you've gotten a lot taller since I last saw you."

William covered his eyes with his fists. "Make her go away."

"Stop that, William," Eric snapped. He pulled William's fists away from his red-rimmed eyes and clasped the narrow wrists in a hand lock.

The child wailed.

Roseann gasped. "Let him go, Eric! You're hurting him."

But Eric wasn't letting up. He clipped his son under the chin. "Look at your grandmother. Go on, say hello."

William dropped his head to his chest. He was heaving, his chest rose and fell spasmodically.

"I *said*, say hello to your grandmother."

"Eric," she cried. "It's okay. Let him be."

"What did I say?"

Sputtering, his nose leaking, William managed a thin "Hel . . . hello."

"That's a lot better." Eric gave the boy's back a push toward the house.

"Wait." Roseann reached into the pocket of her pants and handed a tissue to Eric. "Here, wipe his nose."

"Let's just go inside."

When they stepped into the living room, Roseann turned to her grandson. "I really am glad you're here, William. I've been looking forward all day to seeing you. I went to the store and bought all kinds of games we can play when it's not swimming weather. Do you like to swim? I bet you're a really good swimmer."

The child ignored her. He turned to his father, his eyes so red they looked scorched. "Why are you going away, Daddy?"

"I already told you. I gotta go to the hospital to get something fixed. Come here. Blow."

"Why can't . . . why can't they fix it in the doctor's office? They fixed my finger in the office. I didn't have to stay in the hos . . . hospital."

"William, it's not that kind of fixing," Roseann tried to explain. "Some hurts mean you have to go away for a while. And while your dad is having his hurt fixed, you and I will be together, and we can get to know each other."

William glared at his grandmother. "I don't want to know YOU. I want to be with my mommy. Why can't I stay with her?"

Roseann was about to say that he would be with his mommy in a couple of weeks when Eric interrupted. "You're going to stay with your grandmother. And you will do what I tell you to."

"But where is my mommy?"

"She's away. Okay? And I don't know when she's coming back."

Roseann started. Her mouth formed a little O. Before she had time to ask the question—What did Eric mean that he didn't know when Cindy would be back?—William began wailing again. He pulled Eric's arm. "I gotta pee, Daddy. I can't wait." He crossed his legs and jiggled his body.

"Come with me. Hurry up." Roseann led William down the hallway to the bathroom and shut the door. She and Eric stood side by side outside the bathroom, waiting for the toilet to flush.

Roseann glared at her son and spoke through tight lips. "Where is Cindy? And what do you mean you don't know when she's coming back? You said she was in Boulder, and she was coming in two weeks to get William."

"I don't know that for sure. I haven't been able to reach her."

Roseann fought to swallow her anger. "What do you mean you don't know that for sure?" Her pulse quickened. She could feel it behind her eyes. "You *said* she was coming back. How long am I supposed to be watching William?" She was breathing hard. She hadn't taken her blood pressure pills that morning in her haste to make the flight and was sure her pressure had skyrocketed.

She stepped away from the bathroom so as not to be overhead. Her voice was husky. "You lied to both of us. William thinks his mother is coming for him and you're telling me you don't know where she is. What am I supposed to tell him when he asks why his mother isn't here?"

"Oh, tell him the bitch is in Boulder with that loser! The two of them can go to hell for all I care."

"Lord Jesus." She hated to take the Lord's name in vain, but she couldn't help herself. "You mean Cindy left the two of you? She's deserted you and William? She's in Boulder with a boyfriend? And you don't know when she's coming back?"

"Fuck her, is all I know."

"Eric," she cautioned, placing a finger on her lips, afraid the boy would overhear them.

"Yeah. She's with this guy from work she's been fucking. She's been with him for a year, screwing him behind my back."

Roseann stage-whispered, trying to get Eric to lower his voice, her heart hammering. "You've been lying to me. When you called me and told me to come here, you said Cindy was checking things out. That she'd been offered a promotion and hadn't decided whether to accept the job, and that she'd be coming back for William."

"That's what she told me. For all I know the whole thing is a crock of shit, and she's never coming back. And I wouldn't want her if she came back. Bitch."

Roseann tried to collect her jumbled thoughts. "And do you know how long you'll be away?"

"That depends on the treatment. How I do."

She was almost in tears, "And what am I supposed to do if you're away longer and Cindy never shows up? We have rules here, how long a child can stay. You . . . you should have made it clear, Eric, before

I agreed to help you. You should have told me the whole story. Eric, Eric. What am I to do?"

What was she getting herself into? One more time her son had lied to her. He couldn't be trusted. How did this happen? She and Jack had tried so hard to be decent, good parents, and this is what they got for it. Eric disappointed them time and time again. *Jack, tell me what to do.*

It had taken a while for her and Jack to admit that Eric was a drug addict. He had a long history of drug abuse starting in high school. They had made excuses for his habit until there were no excuses left. He was caught pushing drugs in school and put on probation. He could finish school and get his diploma if he went to rehab. So they'd sent him away.

He was okay for a while, then again and again he turned to drugs. In and out of rehab. Their life was all about Eric. When he was off the drugs, they were filled with hope, only to plunge into despair when he went back to using. Roseann was worried they were using all their savings when their insurance ran out. "Bother the cost," Jack had told her when she cried there would be nothing left for their retirement. "I just want our son clean," he told her. "I know he can do it."

She didn't share Jack's optimism. She blamed the two of them. Somehow, they had failed Eric, and he turned to drugs to fill whatever need they couldn't. Now one more time they were being asked to clean up his mess. Only this time she was alone. The truth was she was sick of having to clean up his mess one more time. Worn out, frazzled, too old to take this on. But now there was William.

Finally, they heard the toilet flush. William came out of the bathroom—his pants were wet. He'd peed all over himself and had been too embarrassed to come out. He cowered next to the door, frightened to show himself.

What was going on in that little head? She bent down and gazed into his blue eyes. Willian was a miniature of Eric at that age. Russet-colored hair, freckles on his little snub nose, a stubborn pointed chin. The mouth was Cindy's, an upside-down parenthesis. William, her grandson. Her heart ached for the child.

"I'm sorry, Daddy. It was an accident."

"What?" Eric studied him. "Jesus Christ, you peed in your pants. What the fuck's wrong with you?"

"Eric, stop it," Roseann demanded. "He said it was an accident. Everyone has accidents, William. Even big folks. Come, Grandma will help you change. We'll unpack your backpack. And then, I bet you're tired and hungry. Did you have any lunch?"

He shook his head no.

"I have some snacks if you are. I could put on the TV, and you could watch one of your programs while your dad and I talk." She bent down and said quietly, like it was a secret they shared, "Maybe you'd be more comfortable if you changed first, huh?"

William seemed to perk up at the idea of watching TV. "I want to play a video game. Can I play games on your TV?"

"No. I'm afraid it's not set up for video games. I have a computer. Maybe you could show me how to set games up on my computer," she said hopefully.

He drew his eyebrows into a line over his blue eyes. "Your computer is probably too old, like your TV."

"Probably," she said.

Eric put his hand on his mother's arm. He seemed to regret treating the kid so hard. "He's a good kid, Mom. He'll be fine. He's not going to be any trouble. This was, well, he doesn't usually behave this way."

"I know that, Eric. It's not that kind of trouble I'm worried about," she said. "Now you go on, William, and go back into the bathroom and get undressed and change your clothes. If you need me, just open the door and I'll come help you. Here's your backpack."

William looked first at his father. "Go on, William. You heard her. I'll never forget this, Mom. I owe you big time."

Roseann removed Eric's hand from her arm. "Go on, William. That's a good boy. What time do you have to check in, Eric?"

"I'm supposed to be there first thing tomorrow."

"I thought you were going straight from here." She looked at her son's eyes. They were glassy. The pupils were small dark pebbles.

"Yeah. I'm going. What choice do I have?"

"I think the choice is pretty clear. At least it was clear to your wife," she said. "And one day it may be clear to William."

"Look, I don't need any of your lectures."

She bit her lip. Eric was right. It was too late for lecturing. She was tempted to ask him to stay the night, but it was better for William if he left right away. It was going to be difficult enough trying to explain to her grandson why his father was leaving him with his grandmother he hardly knew.

"If you're going, you better get started."

Eric knocked on the bathroom door. "Come on out. William. I gotta go now."

The child was naked. Eric grabbed him and pressed him against his chest. The child put one arm around his midsection.

"Sorry I yelled at you. You know I love you, William."

"I love you, too, Daddy."

"Guess this is it, buddy. You're gonna be okay," Eric said, his voice forced, hearty. "Sorry to have to leave you, but I know you and your grandmother are going to have a really great time. She's got lots of things planned, if I know her, and she'll probably cook up a storm. Your grandmother is a really good cook."

"I want to go home. I don't want to stay here with *her*," he mumbled, hugging Eric tighter.

"You're staying, you got that?"

William pulled away from his father and was about to kick his grandmother when Eric grabbed William by the arm and twisted it behind his back.

The child screamed.

"Stop, Eric. Let him go!" Roseann cried.

"Listen up, William. Your grandmother, she's the boss now. You do what she says. That means no back talk, understand? If I hear otherwise, I swear you'll be in big trouble when I get back."

"There's not going to be any trouble, Eric."

"Don't be too soft, Mom. He's got to know who's in charge."

Roseann's stomach was in knots. She turned to the boy. "How about I fix us some dinner, William. I'm pretty hungry and I bet you are too. I was thinking about heating up a pizza."

"I hate pizza."

All kids like pizza. "I bet you like waffles with marshmallow fluff. I know it's a funny kind of dinner but since tonight is special . . ."

"I hate that shit."

"Hey, you watch your mouth."

"He didn't mean it. He's just tired. I think you'd better go, Eric. Now. It's getting late and you have a big day tomorrow. And William, you're as naked as the day you were born. You can't watch TV and eat dinner in the altogether."

William realized he had no clothes on and backed into the bathroom and shut the door.

"He's gotta learn sometime and that sometime is now!"

"Please, Eric. Just go. I'll take care of things."

Eric turned on his heels. "Bye, Mom. I love you."

"I love you," she replied, watching her child, her son, open the door and walk away.

Eric, Eric, she cried inside. *What have you done?*

He revved the motor. The bald tires screeched. The exhaust pipe snaked a dark poisonous trail behind him.

Roseann heard her cell phone ring. She did not answer it. It rang again five minutes later. When she checked recent calls, she saw that both Barbara and Susan had tried to reach her.

Marlene must have called them. All the women in the mah jongg group must know by now what Roseann was up against. Well, she had better things to do than talk on the phone.

William came out of the bathroom. He was wearing a faded Walt Disney World T-shirt and a pair of torn jeans. He ran to look for Eric, then realized he had left.

"Daddy," he wailed. He ran to the window and banged on the pane. He pressed his nose on the glass, fogging an imprint of his mouth. Lifted his head. Screamed, "Daddy! Daddy! Come back!"

Roseann picked up the framed photograph of Eric, Cindy, and William, taken when William was one—a Christmas photo she displayed on a bookshelf that was next to a Hummel figure of a child sitting on his mother's lap. The Hummel figure was her favorite of all the ones her mother collected. She took the figure and put it in her pocket and turned the photo facedown.

CHAPTER THREE

It was a week after the women had gotten together for their weekly mah jongg game, and another workday taking clients around to look at houses. Barbara was exhausted but also exhilarated until she saw her husband's car parked in the driveway. It was two o'clock and she had just left her client at the bank to discuss mortgage options. With luck the young couple would qualify, and Barbara would sell the fixer-upper raised ranch that they wanted but were not sure they could afford. That the bank was trying to work with them was the good news of the day. The bad news was Hank being home in the middle of the day.

She slowed down her pace to the front door weighing the possibilities. Either Hank was sick, or something had gone wrong at work. The fact that he was in perfect health when he left this morning, and in reasonably good spirits, stood in the way of her immediately opening the door. But she couldn't stand there indefinitely, so she took out her key and let herself in.

"Hank, I'm home." Her voice echoed down the dark hallway. Why hadn't he turned on the lights? She hung her coat in the coat closet, went into the kitchen and stood by the sink looking out the window. The pane was frosted, blurring the vista of the barren trees and milking what had been a clear blue sky only hours ago and threatening storm clouds by evening. From the window she could see the cottage she had thought about renting. It needed fixing up, but it would provide some extra income they could use. She'd been meaning to talk to Hank about her idea of renting it.

"Hank, honey, are in you there?" which was a stupid question because she knew very well Hank was in the bedroom.

"Hank?" she repeated. "Honey, I'm coming in."

She moved into the room and saw that Hank was lying in bed, head thrown back, staring up at the ceiling. His camel-hair sports coat was on the easy chair facing the TV on the opposite wall, but he was still dressed in the blue-and white checked shirt and pair of brown tweed pants he'd worn to work. An inch of brown argyle socks peeked out from the cuffs of his pants, an admonishment to her rule that he never put his shoes on the bed.

His gold Rolex, alligator wallet she'd bought him for Christmas, house keys, loose change, and a small canister of weed were on top of the bureau. No mirror, no razor. Thank God.

"Hank." Barbara was close enough to stare into his hazel eyes. His pupils were not dilated, although the telltale smell of alcohol on his breath was cause enough for the ongoing argument about him drinking or getting high in the middle of the day.

"Hank, what's going on?"

He turned away from her toward the wall. "For shit's sake, leave me alone, Barbara."

Undeterred, she sat down on the edge of the bed and touched his shoulder. He shrugged her off.

"Hank," she sighed. She wished it wasn't like this. One more time her heart went out to him. Despite his faults, she knew she'd forgive him. No matter what it was he'd done this time, she loved him and would stand by him.

She wanted to, but didn't dare, trace his mouth and the flat planes of his cheeks and chin with her finger, wanted to caress his brow to smooth away the stress lines and take him in her arms and hold him close. To tell him it doesn't matter. She wasn't ready to give him up.

Whatever it was that had caused Hank to age, that now masked the man she'd fallen in love with and married, she still found him attractive.

Barbara met Hank when they were both juniors at Unity. The fact that Hank had been drawn to her back then when she was a shy willowy blond girl of eighteen, when he could have had any girl in one of the top sororities, amazed, even frightened her. He was a magnet that drew her to him like metal filings. Her resistance was shattered even when she suspected he did not, could not, love her the way she loved him.

They'd met at a fraternity party her roommate had insisted she go to. "You're getting prison pallor from all that studying, Barb. A little fun is what you need. Come on. This frat is supposed to have the best looking guys on campus."

Barbara gave in but her reluctance was evident in the lackadaisical way she had dressed—a pair of old jeans, a washed-out T-shirt under a long-sleeve denim shirt she'd dug out of the laundry basket. The party was in someone's basement and the room was crowded, smoky, noisy. The music blared so loud it was giving her a headache. She suffered migraines and this was the last thing she needed, but her roommate was enjoying herself and she hated to leave her. When she stepped outside to clear her head, she found Hank on his knees struggling to remove a flat tire on the fifteen-year-old Fiat he had bought from a frat brother for three hundred dollars. He cursed the day he ever did. But it was better than riding his bicycle in the snow and rainy weather.

Barbara stood to one side taking it all in. She knew Hank. He was in her chem class, but she'd never spoken to him.

"Fuck," he said, knowing she was there, deliberately ignoring her. Then again, for good measure, he cried "Fuck, fuck," and threw the tire puller on the grass, where it landed two feet away from her.

"Hey, watch it," she screamed, jumping aside.

"Sorry, I didn't mean . . ."

"Okay." She took a step closer and said, "You won't get anywhere without the right tools."

"My roommate, the asshole, took my lug wrench from the trunk and left me this piece of shit."

She bent down, their shoulders nearly touching, to examine the tool that was obviously the problem. "I have one that might work. It's in my car. I could give . . . I mean lend . . . it to you. I assume he left you a spare."

Hank turned his head to face her, sizing her up as one of those smart-ass feminists he'd learned to stay clear of. "Of course, I have a spare. Why else would I need tools to change this?"

Barbara blushed and quickly rose to her feet. "I'll just be a sec." When she returned with the box of tools, he began turning the lug nuts with her wrench without stopping to apologize. She stood by, watching him, while he tugged and groaned, his forehead slick with the effort of tugging and pulling. She couldn't help admiring his muscular arms and the way his dark hair curled at the base of his thick neck. Hank played football for Unity but wasn't what anyone would call a celebrity. Still, the coeds found him irresistible, as women would later in life.

"Thanks," he said, getting up and finally getting a good look at Barbara. "Where's your car. I'll put these back in the trunk."

"That's okay. I think I can manage a toolbox. I brought it over, remember."

He grinned. "Want to go for a beer?"

Barbara didn't drink beer but the chance to spend a little more time with Hank and report back to her roommate was too good a chance to pass up, so she went to the local pub. They were together for two years before getting married, rented a small apartment in New York City, and lived a carefree life as an up-and-coming young couple when Hank landed an entry level job at a well-known advertising company. He rose on the corporate ladder, becoming the director for marketing and advertising, while she taught school. Barbara decided to quit teaching when the high school kids seemed less interested in learning because, she had to admit, she was less interested in teaching them.

Hank was good at his job, but when the three-martini lunches and regular coke habit became a problem, he lost his position and had to settle for working for a much smaller company without the title and prestige he was used to. Barbara got her real estate license and started selling properties in New York and Connecticut. Hank's cut in salary meant adjusting their lifestyle. They decided to leave Manhattan for the burbs and bought a fixer-upper in Connecticut that had a small cottage they had talked about renting out.

It was easier for Barbara to adjust to the changes in lifestyle. It was harder on Hank who liked hand-tailored suits, expensive cars, and mingling with the rich crowd at the golf club. All that had to go when he kept losing his jobs. Never his fault, of course. Barbara was forgiving. She made excuses for him, denied the reality that Hank wasn't going to change his habits for her or anyone else. He still had that "big man on campus" attitude he should have outgrown.

She found she was good at what she did. While Hank's career spiraled downward, hers was advancing upward. She found she was taking control of their marriage, and she liked the feeling of power. Even now, looking at him, she felt less sympathetic than disgusted with his self-indulgent feelings of rejection, his weakness, his denial of what was wrong with him and his refusal to fix what was wrong.

"Hank, what exactly happened?" she asked evenly.

"Fuckin' Dodway said he was sorry, but business was off, we were down clients, and they had to make cuts. I knew it was coming, but I was hoping the Jeffrey account would come through. Thing is, Jeffrey decided to go with digital and social media rather than TV. I tell you Barb, the agency was never up to speed. Not forward-thinking. I shouldn't have gone there in the first place."

"Yes," Barbara said soothingly, "but you were so excited at the time, thinking this was the opportunity you needed to learn more about what you said was personally focused advertising."

"I warned Dodway . . . I warned him. We were missing out. It was that obvious; I don't know why I didn't see it. Thing is, Barb, the fuckin' ignoramus wouldn't listen to me."

Barbara wanted to ask why Hank couldn't just deal with the situation, why he had to be so hot-headed, but she sealed her lips and pretended she understood.

"It's no wonder the agency is going under and taking me with it." Hank sat up and punched his right fist into his left palm. "I hope they all drown, the fuckers."

"Come into the kitchen," Barbara suggested. "I'll make you something to eat. There's not much choice, but I think there's some leftover tuna salad. I could make you a sandwich."

"I'm not hungry." Hank rolled to the other side of the bed, away from her.

"Hank, it will all right. Everything will be all right. This is just a blip on the screen. Things are changing so quickly it's hard to keep up. The ad business is different from when you started, babe. You'll catch up. You just need to give yourself more time."

"Barbara, you don't understand. I am running out of time. I'm fifty-three years old. There are twenty-year-old kids who are making twice what I ever made because they keep on top of things. They look at the data, know what to do with it. They talk a different lingo."

"What about your old clients? The ones who know you and like to work with you?"

"My clients are aging out. There's no interest in traditional advertising. Not like it was. Even TV ads. It's all on your phone. Forget hard copy and that's what I've always done. No, I've got to face it. I'm not in the running anymore. It's fuckin' over."

Barbara flinched as if he'd slapped her. "What's over?"

"This." He was sitting up. He flailed his arms, screwed up his face, his eyes blazing. "This place. We can't afford it. The taxes are killing us. We are over our heads in debt. We're broke, overextended."

She swallowed an accusation over the lump in her throat. *And whose fault is that?* Instead, she said, "Hank, you're just upset. You'll find another job. I know it. I'm going to sell more houses. Work harder. We'll be okay. You'll see."

"Don't do this!" he snarled.

"Don't do what?"

"Make it sound like tomorrow it will all be coming up roses and blue skies. It's not going to get better, Barbara. I'm a loser. I'm not going to get better. And you are not going to save us. You and your pitiful commissions."

"Stop saying that. Just stop it. You're not a loser. And I am one of the best sales agents in my agency. Don't turn away. Hank, do you fuckin' hear me? You're just . . . lost," she said, for lack of a better word.

"Lost?" He laughed. "Like this is some midlife-crisis shit?"

"Oh, come on. You know what I mean."

"Okay, Miss Psychologist. What *do* you mean?"

"I think the time has come for a change and that can be frightening."

He stared at her. "So now I'm afraid of change, is that what you're saying?"

"What I am trying to say is that there comes a time in our life when we need to look ahead, and yes, make changes. Okay, it's not frightening exactly. It's challenging. I think it's time for you to stop working in advertising. Find something else. You're so smart; you can do lots of things."

"Yeah. Like what?'

"Like painting the cottage. Fixing it up so we can rent it. I was thinking we should get a tenant and I even have someone in mind. One of the women in my mah jongg group knows a woman who is looking for place to rent."

"Go to fuckin' hell."

"It's only an idea, Hank. Why not rent the cottage since the kids rarely come to visit and when they do, we can put them up in the house. We can use the extra money and the cottage is so nice. I think we can make a good rental out of it."

When he didn't answer her, Barbara took another tack. "I sold a house today, Hank. There will be a big commission once the sale goes through." She was deliberately exaggerating because her commission wouldn't amount to much on a $350,000 sale.

He shrugged and took off his pants. He exchanged them for a

pair of Calvin Klein jeans and stepped into his new Todd snakeskin loafers. He'd taken off his shirt and stood in front of her, naked from the waist up. He'd put on a bit of weight around the middle, a small paunch, but he still had the body that always turned her on. How she loved making love to him. When was the last time? She knew he was attracted to other women, there had been a number of affairs, but he was hers. She was the one he came home to.

"And there are other clients I am about to sign up. Rich clients who're looking at million-dollar houses. I checked the inventory on Zillow. The market is heating up and there's a whole list of houses I could cobroker with relators I know who would be only too happy to work with me."

He looked past her and went to the window, tapped his fingernail on the glass to discourage a squirrel sprinting up the bird feeder.

Goddamn it, she wanted to scream. *I can keep us afloat while you're changing careers. Changing careers at your age is done all the time.*

Why? Why? Why was he such a failure, she asked herself. It wasn't just the new breed he had to work with; more likely, it was the coke and the drinking. Did he think she hadn't noticed how much he'd been drinking, hiding the empty bottles at the bottom of the trash can and stowing a couple in empty shoe boxes? She was on to him.

"Hank, you haven't answered me about renting the cottage or about fixing it up now that you're home and have the time."

Hank was rummaging through his drawer. "Where the fuck is my black Polo?"

"In the laundry. Sorry, but I didn't get to do the wash. And Hannah isn't coming until Wednesday. Hank, please, what about my idea about renting the cottage? I don't know what it would go for, but I could easily find out. And there is this potential renter. What do you think? Should we rent it? Furnished, we could get more, but if there is interest in it unfurnished, we could probably store most of the stuff in our basement and garage."

She realized she was getting way ahead of herself, trying to sort out the possibilities, already composing a rental listing in her head if the woman Marlene had told her about turned out not to be interested. Lovely bright—no, airy—two-and-a-half-room cottage in private wooded area, a short distance from town. Freshly painted with small, efficient kitchen . . .

"Hank?" she looked at him hopefully.

He'd changed into his second-best black T-shirt. "I'm going out for a while."

She flinched as if he'd slapped her across the face. "Where are you going? You haven't eaten. I was going to make you a sandwich. And you haven't said anything about my idea."

"I'll grab something in town. Do what you want. You always do anyway. Don't wait up."

"What do you mean, "Don't wait up," she cried, panic in her voice. "Please, honey, stay home. I need you to stay home with me. Don't go."

He brushed past her and left her standing by the front door, watching him drive off in his Boxster convertible they were still paying off. It was midafternoon. Too much time to be alone, worried about the future.

She picked up her cell phone planning to call the clients she'd dropped off at the bank to see if they had gotten the mortgage. She changed her mind. If they hadn't, she couldn't face any more bad news today. Maybe she would go back to the office and finish up some paperwork.

Susan had texted, reminding the women they'd be playing at her house next Tuesday and to come early since she would be ordering sandwiches.

The last thing in the world Barbara wanted was to play mah jongg and to have to face her friends. If she went, which she wasn't planning on, she wasn't going to say anything about Hank being out of work. But she might mention the availability of the cottage.

She clicked Susan's number. Busy as usual. She left a message that she wasn't sure she was coming Tuesday, and she would let her know later in the week. "Something has come up at work," she lied. "See if you can get a sub. Again, I'm sorry to have to miss the game but I'm sure you'll understand. And what about that woman you mentioned who is looking for a place to stay. Is she still interested? I've decided to list the cottage."

Determined to go ahead, she reread the listing and posted it on the agency's website. Just in case the woman Susan mentioned was no longer a possibility, she wanted to move forward. *You have to be prepared for all contingencies by just making life adjustments.* Something her father had driven into her head when she complained about things not going her way. She was ready to make whatever adjustments were called for, even if Hank wasn't.

CHAPTER FOUR

Grace hadn't planned on moving from the apartment she shared with Noreen, a student she'd met in grad school They were both getting degrees in clinical social work and in the beginning the two women got along famously. Grace once read that some people are pushed and others are pulled into making changes. Grace did not fear change, in fact she rather liked it, she just was not ready to move to another place with so many other changes going on in her life. She supposed she was pushed because Noreen, who really was a nice person, played her music until all hours of the night. When Grace came home from her graveyard stint at the VA, where she was interning, the last thing she wanted to hear before she fell asleep was Bob Marley and reggae music, which she otherwise quite enjoyed.

Grace could forgive Noreen, who also had to unwind after working with difficult clients during the day. Unfortunately, the walls between their bedrooms were thin, and Grace was a light sleeper. She could barely keep her eyes open the next day from lack of sleep. The other problem was Noreen's laissez fair attitude toward housekeeping. She rarely unloaded the dishwasher, and when she did, she still left dirty dishes in the sink. Most annoying was the habit she had of helping herself to the food Grace kept in the refrigerator, even though her apology notes were sincerely written. *Gosh, I was starving, and your chicken salad was so tempting, I could not resist eating it since it looked like it was going bad.*

Grace did not have the heart to ask her to repay her or at least replenish the food she ate. They both were on a shoestring budget.

Susan was in Grace's yoga class. One day when Grace was so exhausted, she was barely able to finish the class, she confessed to Susan that her living situation was hell.

Susan told her about Barbara's cottage. "I don't know if Barbara has listed it yet, but I bet she'd be willing to let you see it."

"How much is she asking?"

"I'm not sure, but if I put in a good word, she might come down in price. She's eager to get the right person since the cottage is so close to their house. She and her husband Hank live next door. I've known Barbara for years. She's a real estate agent."

"What about her husband?"

"To tell you the truth, I don't know much about him except he seems to be spending a lot more time working around the place."

That evening, Susan called Barbara. "I think I've got the perfect tenant for your cottage. Grace is a clinical social worker. She's a single mother. Her twin boys are in college, so you won't have to deal with kids."

Barbara was eager to meet Grace and a showing was scheduled two days later.

Grace was nervous. She arrived a few minutes before the time was set to see the cottage. She was still wearing the long sleeve white button-down shirt and black pants she had worn to work. She always dressed simply. Her only adornment was a colorful silk scarf she tucked under her collar and large hoop earrings that glittered against her bronze skin.

Barbara had just come from work herself. She was in one of her foul moods because the couple she'd been working with for almost a year jumped ship and went to another agency. Barbara learned the couple had bid on a two-million-dollar house by the beach. The other broker turned out to be the owner of the beach house and kept the entire commission.

When Grace rang the doorbell to the main house, it was Barbara who opened the door.

"Hello. I'm Grace, Susan's friend. I called about the cottage."

"Yes, I know. Just a sec and I'll get the key." She looked over her shoulder to see if Hank, watching TV in the back room, had heard the bell, but if he had he was not curious enough to come out of the room to see who was here.

"Susan spoke very highly of you," Grace said following her across an uneven flagstone path to the cottage. She had to watch her step on the broken stones half sunken in the muddy craters. "Susan said you were in her mah jongg group. I know nothing about the game, but it has always fascinated me. Is the cottage still available?"

"I only just listed it and already there have been lots of inquiries," Barbara lied.

Grace's face fell. "Oh, I hope I'm not too late then."

Barbara wished she could take back her ploy, which was to get Grace to act quicky.

"The cottage is rather small. There's a kitchenette, open-space living room, dining area, and a small bedroom. I'm not sure it would work as an office to see clients if that's what you're planning."

"Oh, I'm not planning to open a private practice just yet. Possibly down the line." Grace was worried she'd ruin her chances of getting the cottage if she admitted that seeing private clients was her plan, assuming she had any, which right now she didn't. "For now I want to find a quiet place where I can unwind. I love my work, but it can be stressful and when I come home, I want to relax in peace and quiet. I love the surrounding woods. Yet it's not that far from town, close enough that I can ride my bicycle if I feel the need for civilization."

Barbara smiled. "It's quiet enough. It's just my husband and me. Our daughter lives in California and doesn't visit that often."

"My twin boys are away at college and will only come to visit during semester breaks and perhaps a week at a time during the summer."

"By the way, were you thinking furnished or unfurnished?"

"I have my own furniture, dishes, and linens. And I have some things in storage I would like to use. Storage is so expensive. May I see the cottage now?"

"Well, this is it," Barbara said, turning the key. The smell of fresh paint and turpentine wafted through the doorway.

Grace stopped in the small vestibule. She held her breath taking in the pegged floors, the pickled pine wood cabinets in the kitchenette, the oversized farm sink, and the four-burner stove—the white-enamel surface gleaming—everything so bright, clean, and inviting. She wanted to hug the room. "It's wonderful," she gushed, picturing herself having her morning tea while seated at her round red vintage Formica table with the chrome chairs and red vinyl seats.

"You haven't seen the rest." Barbara pointed to the wall in the living room. "My husband Hank built the cabinets and shelves with barn wood. He is pretty handy if you need something fixed." They went into the bathroom. "We plan on replacing the bathroom tub. It's an ancient claw-foot soak tub we inherited when we bought the place ten years ago. The sink has been replaced and there's plenty of hot water."

"Oh, leave it," Grace cried running her palm along the rim of the tub. "It's wonderful."

"I'm afraid we've focused on renovating the main house. There's still a lot to do with the cottage."

"I'm handy myself and I own a well-stocked tool kit."

"Well, that's good to know."

Bending over the tub, Grace was able to see the view of the sugar maples. "The trees are glorious. I wonder how old they are."

"I have no idea," Barbara said. "Here's the bedroom. It's small but you can just fit a queen-size bed."

"I have a double, so that won't be a problem." Grace turned to Barbara. Her eyes were sparkling. Her cheeks were flushed. "This is absolutely perfect. I'd love to live here." Tingling with excitement she waited impatiently for Barbara to say something. To tell her how much it would cost her. Probably way too much for her to afford. She made a silent prayer to the rental gods to let her have the place.

Barbara couldn't help liking the woman. She was ready to let Grace have the cottage. She liked her enthusiasm and had the feeling she would take good care of the place. But shouldn't she ask Hank to meet Grace before agreeing to rent her the cottage? After all, they would be living in proximity. He should be part of the decision. Yet Hank had made it clear that he wasn't interested in whether she rented the cottage or not. You always do what you want anyway, he'd said.

She considered the pluses and minuses of renting Grace the cottage.

Plus: Grace was a professional. Susan had been so impressed with her, she'd told her about the cottage. She would vouch for Grace.

Minus: What did she know about this woman other than that she worked for a social service agency and couldn't be making much money. Could she afford the rent she'd be asking? Also, she hadn't interviewed anyone else.

Plus: Grace had expressed some interest in learning how to play mah jongg when Barbara told her about her steady Tuesday game.

Grace bit her bottom lip. She'd said, "I would love to, but I don't know how to play."

"Well, I could loan you my mah jongg card until you get your own and you could go online and read how to play. That is if you want to . . ." She let the idea hang in the air.

"Sure," Grace replied. "It sounds like fun. I'd love to learn. And it will be a nice break from dealing with clients and their problems."

"Fantastic," Barbara gushed. "I'm sure it won't take you long to catch on."

A new mah jongg player to fill in when they needed a sub. The cottage deal was sealed on the spot.

CHAPTER FIVE

The next week when the group was meeting to play mah jongg at her place, Susan greeted Marlene at the door. Marlene's cheeks were rosy and her hair a whirlwind unfettered from its usual ponytail. She was breathing hard, having opted to climb the three flights of stairs in her endeavor to drop a few pounds.

"Am I late?"

"Actually, you're fifteen minutes early. I just finished putting on my makeup."

Marlene thrust a white paper sack in her direction. "Do you mind if I put this in your refrigerator?"

"No. What is it?"

"Halibut. The reason I'm late."

Susan caught a whiff of the fishy smell and pinched her nostrils.

"I stopped off at Foster's for some halibut to make for dinner. The fish you get in the supermarket is farm raised. His is really fresh. Foster's is more expensive but worth it, don't you think?"

Without speaking, Susan went into the kitchen and opened the refrigerator and pointed to the second shelf.

"Thanks. Don't let me forget it."

"I won't."

Marlene took off her damp yellow rain jacket and put it on the back of one of the folding chairs around the card table set up in the living room. She sank into the deep persimmon couch under the picture window that offered a view of maple trees aflame in the fall but dark as pitch all winter. It had rained steadily for six days, and everyone, especially Marlene, who only loved the outdoors when she could, as she put it, play in the flower and vegetable gardens. Everyone felt waterlogged. But at least it wasn't snow.

"Let me hang that up," Susan said, keeping the jacket at arms' length. Even the jacket smelled fishy.

"Whatever do you do with your car? I must've circled the block a zillion times until I found a spot."

"There's a parking garage around the corner, Marlene. You can't miss it."

"I suppose." Marlene shrugged her shoulders. "That's new. The lamp with the . . . don't tell me it's real Tiffany?" Marlene had been to Susan's place lots of times to play mah jongg, but since Susan was perpetually redecorating, there was always something new to take in. The furnishings, for the most part, were ultramodern with a smattering of antiques, not at all to her or Al's taste, which ran to colonial (his preference) and hand-me-downs.

"No, it's a reproduction," Susan lied, not wanting to put on airs. It was one of the pieces she insisted on having from the second divorce, and she had recently taken it out of storage. One of many fine pieces she felt she deserved for putting up with the latest ex who didn't mind giving it up. He, like Susan, was into interior design. She supposed that was the attraction that had kept the marriage together until it was time to redecorate—including a change of spouses.

"New decorator," she explained to Marlene. "She believes a home must be *holistically aesthetically balanced*."

"Is that so? I'm not sure what that means. I suppose Al's and my taste is more like 'keep things the way they are until they have moth holes.'"

Susan smiled sweetly. She glanced around the living room and adjusted the lampshade Marlene had admired that was minutely askew. The cleaning woman had been there the day before, more focused on the dust than the room's aesthetic balance. "I'd offer you something to eat, but I'm waiting for the sandwiches and dessert platters to be delivered."

"Oh, you really didn't have to bother, Susan. We could have brought our own sandwiches. And heavens, we could do without the calories. Cheese and fruit would be more than enough. You are setting the bar too high for the rest of us."

"Nonsense. Would you like something to drink? I have mineral water or Diet Coke."

"A glass of tap water with some ice would be fine."

Susan returned to the kitchen, opened two small bottles of Perrier, one for Marlene and one for herself, and put some ice cubes in each glass, wondering if she should broach the subject that had been bothering her since they played mah jongg at Marlene's, when Al had made them feel so unwelcome and Marlene rushed them out of the house.

Marlene was thumbing through a recent copy of *Architectural Digest*. "When you're done with this, may I borrow it?"

"Of course, Marlene." Susan geared herself up before she began. She inhaled and exhaled and said quietly, "Marl, I hope you don't mind, but I was wondering if . . . if you . . . well, if you ever gave a thought to how much Al seems to dominate your life?" There, she said it.

"Excuse me?" Marlene looked up from the article on pool landscaping. She wasn't sure she had heard Susan correctly and leaned forward, staring at Susan, who was nibbling her bottom lip. "Did you just say something about my Al dominating my life?"

"What I meant, Marlene, is that in some ways Al has control over you—the time you spend with your friends, what you do, your way of looking at things."

"Control?" Marlene repeated, her voice rising. She was so taken aback by the accusation she could hardly find the words to retaliate. "Control over me?" she sputtered. "Are you comparing me to one of those women in the Middle East countries whose husbands take away their freedom? That I have no life of my own because I'm married?"

Susan took a sip of her Perrier. "That's not exactly how I would put it. But you do have to admit, Al really does run the show and, as a result, you lack a certain independence."

"Independence? Susan, Al is the center of my life. We are bonded for life. We care deeply about one another."

"I didn't mean to imply . . ."

Marlene folded her arms across her chest tight with indignation. "Oh, I know what you are implying, Susan. That Al is controlling. That I don't have a life of my own. But you're wrong. What you fail to realize is that I enjoy doing things for Al. I don't feel dominated. I feel loved."

Susan was about to say that being bonded by love was all very well, but maybe that bond was too restricting, when, thankfully, the doorbell buzzed. "That must be our sandwiches."

Marlene was still in shock. She had to sit down, or she was going to faint. *How dare she. Of all the nerve!* So that was what the other women were also thinking! They were examining her relationship with Al under a microscope. The very idea brought tears to her eyes. She had never felt so humiliated, so offended by what Susan and the others must be saying behind her back.

The delivery boy carried the cellophane-covered trays of sandwiches and cookies into the kitchen. Right behind him were Barbara and Grace. "I'll be right in," Susan told them. The game is set up in the living room."

Susan signed the receipt—she used the office credit card—and gave the boy a generous tip.

"Hi, Marlene," Grace said, sensing something in the air when Marlene didn't bother to greet them. "Mar, is something the matter?" Grace asked. "Your cheeks are flushed."

Marlene shook her head, trying to hold back her tears, deciding if she should get her fish, ask for her raincoat, and quit the game. But how would that look? And then they would only have three to play since Roseann was still away. Also, wouldn't it suggest that Susan had the upper hand? She couldn't allow that. Instead, she began turning over the tiles.

"Mar?" Grace repeated when Marlene sniffled.

"It must be Susan's cat. I'm highly allergic to cats."

"Oh, I'm sorry, Marlene. Actually, my cat is at the vet, and I thought the cleaning women had vacuumed all the hair. Well, now that we are all here, how about we begin. Would you prefer to eat while we play or eat first?" Susan asked.

"Since I can only play until three, how about we eat while we play," Barbara suggested.

The women agreed and immediately began building the walls against their racks when Grace asked if there'd been any news from Florida. Marlene said she'd talked to Roseann that morning. "She's very nervous the condo board is checking how long William has been staying with her. He can only stay ninety-one days."

"Hopefully, his parents will come for him before his time is up," said Susan, wishing she hadn't said what she did to Marlene.

"It doesn't look that way. There's been no word from Cindy, and Roseann told me Eric cut out of his rehab program. He hasn't called, and she is worried sick that he could be suicidal."

"That's awful." Grace wrinkled her brow. "Is there any way of tracing his whereabouts?"

"She's not about to go to the police, if that's what you mean," Marlene snapped. "Sorry, Grace, I'm feeling a bit low myself right now."

Susan was East. She reached for the dice and counted the number of tiles that would be in the hot wall, then distributed the rest to begin the Charleston. "Imagine taking care of an eight-year-old at our age?" she remarked, arranging her suits. She had three Jokers, which made it more difficult to figure out which hand to play. The play began when she discarded her extra tile, a one Bam. The women ate their sandwiches and sipped their drinks while they played. Nothing interfered with their concentration when it came to mah jongg, although one time one of the women Susan played with at another game fell off her chair and fainted dead away. The three others had complained about having to forfeit their good hands while they waited for the medics.

"These are delicious." Grace wiped her fingers on a paper napkin each time she was about to pick up a tile. "I may just go back for a second—bother the waistline."

"Where did you order from?" Barbara wanted to know.

"Oh, it's just a local catering service our office uses," she told the women. She neglected to say that she no longer worked for Dr. Malcolm or the reason she was let go, but she'd held on to the office credit card—which she deserved after what she'd had to put up with! "Would anyone like something more to drink? There are cookies too."

The women agreed they were fine and that Susan was to stop being a hostess and just play.

Grace won the first game. It was a concealed hand that won her fifty cents from each player. She collected the winnings and put them in her change purse.

"That's kind of cute," Marlene commented, trying to lift her spirits by pretending an interest in the purse's patchwork design.

"It's a gift from one of my clients. She's back in the hospital."

Barbara set up her wall and after tossing the dice began distributing the tiles to the women to hurry things along.

"I really admire your dedication," Susan said, disapproving of the way Barbara was taking control of the tile distribution. Each woman was supposed to take her tiles in turn. "I don't know how you do it, Grace."

"Obviously, she isn't doing it for the money," Marlene said, glancing at her tiles she'd arranged on her rack.

Barbara turned to Grace. "If you are, I will have to raise your rent. Just kidding. You know how delighted I am to have you as my tenant."

"And I am *delighted* to have you as a landlord and friend," Grace replied. "I can't believe my luck, living in such a lovely place and having you and Hank next door." She pressed Barbara's hand and smiled.

The game progressed at a slow pace while the women ate their food and played.

"Grace, please throw a tile," Marlene said. She felt a bit better when she was playing mah jongg and concentrating on her hand. It was the best therapy when feeling low, unless someone you were playing with was dumping on your husband.

Marlene selected a tile from her rack admiring the details of the tiles Susan had recently purchased along with a new mah jongg set embossed with gold lettering. That made her fourth set if she counted correctly, while she was still playing with her mother's vintage set.

"Four Bam. I've been asked to take on some contract work at Crofton Family Services," Grace announced. "One of the social workers went on maternity leave and I was asked to take over her caseload."

"Does that mean you are no longer considering seeing patients privately?" Barbara asked. She'd been thinking about asking Grace if she would stop by to see Hank, although she wasn't sure Hank would go for it. It might be a little awkward, Hank talking to Grace about his work issues. On the other hand, she mused, Hank seemed to like Grace and maybe if she just casually suggested he and Grace meet, Grace being a vocational counselor as well as a clinical social worker . . .

Grace rearranged the array of tiles on her rack. She had two Jokers, and now she'd just picked a third. This should make it easy to complete her pattern. She was one away from mah jongg. "I am beginning to see patients privately. It is far more lucrative. The work at the clinic is more like paid volunteering."

"Then why do it?" Marlene was trying very hard not to obsess about Susan's earlier remarks, but the comment about Al being controlling and her lack of independence was like a wasp's sting.

"I really like the clients I see at the clinic; they're very challenging. Most of them are homeless with psychiatric disorders. Once they are stabilized, we find them places to live and give them vocational training, so they can rejoin the work force. There's a terrible stigma about mental illness. I wish we could do more to educate the public." Grace sighed, fingering the tiny stiches of the change purse where the fabric was sewn by the client in her arts and crafts therapy class. If only the woman's disjointed life could be so easily patched. "So sad. I had such great hopes for her."

"What happened to put her in the hospital?"

"She stopped taking her meds, decompensated, and had to be involuntarily admitted because she threatened to hurt herself."

"What a shame." Marlene frowned.

"I'm not supposed to talk about my clients, but this one is a real love."

Susan picked up a tile and added it to the mosaic. "South."

"How did you know she stopped taking her meds?" Marlene asked.

"It's easy to tell when you see the abrupt changes in behavior. She was always particular about her appearance. Never a hair out of place, nails manicured every week."

"Sounds like someone we know," Marlene muttered.

Susan glowered at Marlene and slammed her rack, rattling the tiles embossed with her initials that, miraculously, did not fall to the floor. "Would you stop needling me, Marlene? I apologize if I offended you earlier."

"Accepted," Marlene said halfheartedly. "Go on with your story, Grace."

Barbara was checking the card while Grace continued talking. Should she try a concealed hand since this one seemed doomed? She did not know what to throw.

"Barb, you are holding up the game," Marlene reminded her.

"Sorry."

"To answer your question, Marlene," Grace said, I knew as soon as she walked in to see me that she was in trouble. So unlike herself: her hair like a rat's nest and wearing a soiled nightgown. When I went to see her, she could barely control her palsy. I assume they're giving her a high dose of lithium—I'll take that four Dot you threw, Barbara—yet she'd managed to make me the change purse you admired, Marlene, which says something positive about the treatment she's getting. At least she wasn't sitting in her room just staring at the wall." Grace paused and counted her tiles. "Hmmm. I do believe I have mah jongg. Twenty-five cents each, please."

Susan shifted her weight in her chair and felt her cellphone vibrate. Since their decision to keep the phones on mute, she was constantly trying to detect a vibration. And here it was. But she doubted the players would let her get up now to see who was trying to reach her.

"How is your mom doing, Marlene?" Grace asked, adding the change to her winnings.

"Worse. The chemo treatment is finished, and next week she starts her rounds of radiation. I'll be taking turns with my sister driving her to the hospital, so I'm not sure I'll be able to play if she has an appointment on a Tuesday."

"In which case we can always change the day to help you," Susan said.

"Some of us work," Barbara said bitterly, thinking about the argument she'd had with Hank this morning. They were always arguing about something. She didn't know how much she could take. You were supposed to relax and have fun playing mah jongg with your friends, but so far, she hadn't won a single game and now there was talk of changing their day to accommodate Marlene.

"Barbara?" Susan looked at her. "Don't you agree we could change our day to help Marlene out?"

"No, I don't. If I am meeting a client, I am not about to ask the client to change our appointment because one of the players has a conflict. Our day is Tuesday. That's the day I blocked out on my calendar . . . Marlene, are you playing or what? You're East."

"I'm sorry. I just have so much on my mind. Everything seems to fall on me. My dad is no help at all."

"Maybe he's overwhelmed. Not everyone can be a caretaker. It might be easier for everyone if your mom lived with you and Al for a while," suggested Grace.

"Al and I talked about it. We offered to have Mom stay with us, but she refuses to leave her house. All she does is complain about my father, how difficult he is, that he is just waiting for her to die so he can get on with his life." This time she allowed the tears to flow.

"How awful for you, Marlene, to have to listen to that bullshit," Susan said.

Marlene continued to weep. "I'm sorry . . ."

"Ladies, ladies, too much chatter. Some of us should leave our troubles at home and just play mah jongg," Barbara griped as Marlene continued to sob.

"It's all this talking about your mom." Grace placed her hand over Marlene's. It was warm and firm.

Susan rested her elbows on the table and felt the phone in her pants pocket vibrate again. *Damn. I can't get up now.* She looked at her friends and felt a pang of sorrow for each of them: Barbara putting up with Hank. Something was heating up there, she could tell, although Barbara was very private about her home life. And here was Grace, who was obviously worried about money. Perhaps she wasn't as happy living next door to Barbara as she let on. Susan knew that Hank was a problem with his drinking and whatever. Grace must hear him sounding off since the cottage was not that far from the main house. And poor Marlene, married to the chauvinist Al, was taking care of her sick mom. What a sad state she was in. And then there was Roseann, stuck in Florida with her grandson who'd apparently been abandoned by his mother and father.

Susan was on the verge of telling Barbara how wrong she was about wanting the women to keep their troubles to themselves. The underlying mission in getting together was caring for one another. Yes, they played a game that had been around for centuries that called for skill and luck. But their game had begun to take on a new meaning as they'd gotten to know each other more. This was an opportunity to bond, to learn about each other and to support one another. There might be a day when they were too old to recognize or recall the names of the tiles (god forbid), but the friendship they'd formed was bound to be long-lasting. This was far more important than winning or losing at mah jongg.

Susan looked around. It had been a difficult day for some of the players, but they had come to play mah jongg anyway. What the women needed was cheering up.

"Now, ladies," she said brightly. "I have just the thing to lift our spirits. Literally."

With that she went into the kitchen, opened the refrigerator, and gagged. The fish stank to high heaven and would ruin whatever leftovers she had from last night's dinner with the man she'd said she would not see again, but relented and spent another evening bored to tears. Not only did she wind up paying for her dinner, but he'd tried to fuck her in the back of his car. At her age. At least have the decency to invite her back to his house or suggest they go to her place.

She really had to forget about those dating sites. *Give it a rest.* Curious, she glanced at the number that had been calling her. Gary Rheingold. Maybe she'd ping him back when the game ended.

Ah, nice and cold. She removed the bottle and wrapped it in a dishtowel. Next, she opened a cabinet and took down four Tiffany crystal flutes. She'd bought the flutes with Dr. Malcolm's credit card, justifying the purchase as another office expense when he asked about the charge. "To toast us," she teased, knowing he reveled in their after-hours trysts and would deny her nothing until his wife caught on to their affair.

Susan carried everything into the living room where three sets of eyes widened when they saw what she was about to do.

"Are you out of your mind?" Marlene gasped, seeing the label on the bottle. *Dom Perignon?* She had heard of but never tasted the champagne. Even at their wedding, so many years ago, her father had toasted the bride and groom with prosecco.

"I don't think so. We deserve the best." Susan popped the cork and a spray of champagne rose over the mah jongg table. Carefully, she poured the bubbly into the flutes. "I've had it with listening to nothing but problems, problems, problems."

"It has become quite a shit show." Barbara lifted her flute, the bubbles like golden dewdrops. She wet her lips in anticipation.

"Shouldn't we try to get ahold of Roseann? We could Zoom or WhatsApp her," Marlene suggested. "I hate to leave her out."

"By the time she figures out how to get onto those sites, the bubbles will be flat," Susan replied.

"Maybe William could show her how to log on," Marlene offered.

"I wouldn't count on it," Barbara and Susan said in unison.

Grace lifted her glass and embraced her mah jongg friends with her whole heart. "Here's to the shine, dear ones."

"Drink up," Susan sang out.

"To us. To us. To us." Clink went the glasses.

CHAPTER SIX

William did not look up when his grandmother put the bowl of grapes on the coffee table in front of him. Stretched out on the couch, his head propped on the arm, he stared straight ahead at the screen of the old television she hadn't replaced with one of the newer ones she'd been meaning to buy. While this one didn't have rabbit ears, it might as well have since she didn't have cable, but she did have a DVD player, so they had borrowed some videos discs from the library.

William was watching cartoons. While Roseann didn't approve of the violence of some of them—there was always someone getting blown to smithereens and the noise was earsplitting—she was glad there was something to take his mind off his situation.

Because William liked her meatballs and spaghetti, they were having it for the second time that week. She grabbed a handful of pasta and put it in the boiling water. William did not like eating vegetables; nevertheless, she looked in the freezer for a package of peas.

"Eat your vegetables and you can stay up a half hour past your bedtime to watch TV."

"I'd rather have a new game," he'd bargained when she made that offer.

Roseann laughed. She'd already bought two games he downloaded on his phone and played under the covers when she sent him to bed.

It took three calls for William to come to the table. Roseann sat across from him, watching her grandson twirl the spaghetti on his fork. His mouth was rimmed with red, like a cardinal's beak, while he slurped her homemade tomato sauce. Without his asking, she refilled his bowl with a second helping.

"I hope there's room for strawberry ice cream," she said, clearing the bowl he'd wiped clean with his finger.

"Got any sprinkles?"

"Of course."

William was safe, happy. Healthier. In the time he'd been with her, his face was rounder and he'd lost that faraway, forlorn, abstracted look he'd had when he first came. She didn't want anything to destroy that sense of security, even though she knew it might not last. Time was running out. Ninety-one days was the longest he could stay according to the community rules, and then William would have to leave Sundial Acres. Was it her imagination that someone on the board was counting the days?

Why hadn't Eric or Cindy called?

Her cell rang. Each time it did, her heart leaped, thinking that finally she would get word. But it was only Marlene who wanted to give her an update on her mom who had been diagnosed with pancreatic cancer. Marlene still couldn't get over the shock and had a need to talk. Roseann was usually sympathetic, but she had her own problems now to deal with.

Roseann used to look forward to Marlene's calls, but now she dreaded them because they reminded her of her old life: mah jongg with friends who gossiped and laughed. When she'd been able to forget her problems and concentrate on completing a pattern according to the mah jongg card. When all that was required was skill and luck.

"Hello Rosie."

"Marlene." Disappointment filled her chest. "Wait a minute." She looked at William, who was gathering the pieces for the sky of the five-hundred-piece puzzle they were working on and went out on the porch to talk.

"Oh, Marlene." Roseann's voice broke. "There's still no word."

"Rosie, shall I come? My sister is coming to take care of Mom, so I'll have a break to stay with you."

"No, good God, no. Don't come. But thank you, Marlene. You have enough on your plate without taking on my problems."

"Are you sure you're okay?"

"Really, I'm fine, Marlene. I'm glad your sister is coming. How is Mom?"

"Not so good. But I don't want to talk about her now. This week we played at Susan's, and we were all saying how worried we were about you. Our new player Grace offered to find out about your local social services for when you come home if Eric still hasn't appeared. Arrangements will have to be made for William."

Roseann flinched. She inhaled, trying to control her fury. Her heart was palpitating like a tom-tom. *The nerve of that woman, Grace.* They hadn't met but here she was interfering in her affairs.

"You tell Grace that's the last thing I need. I don't want some child-welfare lady poking her nose into my business. It's bad enough worrying night and day about the board members breathing down my neck without getting social services involved if I bring William back with me."

"How long has he been with you?"

"I told you, two and a half months." The time pressed on Roseann like a fifty-pound weight.

"Sorry, half the time I feel as if I'm walking in a fog. I'm so worried about Mom."

"I understand," Roseann said, trying to be sympathetic when her own life was filled with worry about William.

"And what about school? Are you taking him to school?"

"I visited the school principal and explained the situation. She had me meet with the school psychologist, and when I said I was taking care of William until his parents came for him, and that I was planning on homeschooling until we sorted things out, she agreed that sounded like the best temporary arrangement, especially after talking to William, who said he wanted to be with me. It was too far to drive William to school every day, I said. This seemed like the best solution.

"The school was very understanding. I had to file some papers proving I was the grandmother and that I was responsible for William—for the time being—and that Eric had left William in my care. I picked up the books he needs, and the teachers give me his work. Every other week I report back, and they give me new assignments." There was a long silence on the other end. Roseann felt compelled to add, "And William is doing just fine. He seems to like the arrangement. He is so bright, Marlene. You can't imagine."

"So now, in addition to being a full-time babysitter, you are his teacher. Roseann, listen to yourself. This is absolute madness."

"No, it makes complete sense, Marlene. Look, I don't mind the teaching although, I admit, I have a lot of catching up to do. Especially in math." She laughed. "Never my best subject fifty years ago."

Marlene sighed. "The game is at my house this week, although I'm never sure what the week will bring. It's so up and down with Mom being so sick. What should I tell the women?"

"I don't care what you tell them. I'm doing whatever is needed to protect William. I don't want him taken from me, and I'm not sure he's better off with his parents."

"Grandma! I need you." William's voice was insistent.

"Roseann, if you change your mind about me coming . . ." she offered doubtfully, knowing she really should be around for her mother.

"Grandma!"

"Sorry, I have to go. Don't worry so much. I'm fine. We both are."

Roseann clicked off her cellphone and hurried into the house. "What's wrong, William?"

"Some pieces are missing."

Roseann sighed. "It looks like you lost two for the sky."

"I know."

"Did you look under the couch?"

William got down on his hands and knees. "Oh, I found them." William fitted the puzzle pieces into the empty spaces.

"Great. Now you should work on the river."

"Who were you talking to, Grandma?"

"Aunt Marlene. She says hello. Do you remember Aunt Marlene?"

He pouted. "I thought maybe you were talking to Daddy."

"No, William." Roseann began sorting the pieces for the river, the ripples of blue and aqua, some glistening with sunlight. "But I'm sure we'll hear from him soon."

William got up and tipped the table so the puzzle pieces fell on the floor, then he ran outside. Roseann ran after him. *William, William.* When she finally caught up with him, she was out of breath. She held him to her, her heart pounding. "I know, I know," she soothed. "It hurts. It hurts really, really bad. William, I know all about pain. Pain is a wound, but it will heal. Please, come into the house before anyone sees us."

William went to bed early. He did not try to play his games. Instead, he buried his head in his pillow and cried until there were no more tears left in his ragged body. Roseann listened to his sobs and cried silent tears with him.

That night he crept into her bed. She wrapped her arms around him and breathed in the sour musky boyish odor mingled with rejection and fear.

The next day she tried calling Cindy but the number she had had been disconnected. She doubted Cindy was in Boulder. She left messages on Eric's cell. He did not call back.

That night, when they were reading a book for science about parts of the body, William asked, "What part of my daddy is getting fixed?" Roseann fumbled for the right response.

"Well, it's a kind of part of the mind that tells you how to behave," she tried explaining, hoping she wouldn't have to go into great detail.

"Where is that part?"

"It's the psychological part of the brain that we call your conscience."

"That part tells you how to be good?"

"Exactly. How to not get into trouble, and to do what you are supposed to do and to listen to good advice."

"That is a dumb part of the body to fix."

"Not really. Some people have to learn how to break bad habits. Like to stop taking too many pills or drinking too much alcohol that makes them . . ."

"Angry at me and Mommy."

"Yes, to control your temper."

"To use your words like Mrs. Rothstein used to tell us. To not fight or use the f-word."

Roseann looked into William's eyes, trying to find the right way to explain Eric's frightening outbursts. "If your dad forgets to use his words sometimes, I want you to remember that he still loves you." Her voice dropped, smothered in pain and years of grief. "To remember that your dad . . . he loves you so much and he loves your mom . . . and I just know he wants to do better for the two of you and that's why he went away this time and . . ." even more softly, "stays away."

William's eyes blazed with fury. "That's a lie. That's a lie. Daddy doesn't love Mommy and Mommy doesn't love him anyways."

"That's not true, William."

"Yes, it is. I heard her tell Daddy she hates him, and she wants nothing to do with him. I heard her say that; I really did. I'm not making it up, Grandma." His eyes filled with tears, and he swiped them with his fist.

Roseann held out her arms and he came into them, pressed his head against her heaving chest. "Oh, I don't think you would make that up, William. I'm sure you wouldn't. I know it can make us very sad and worried when adults get so angry that they say things they don't really mean. Your mommy, well, she might have said that once—"

"She said that a couple of times; she did, she did," he insisted.

Roseann couldn't respond. There wasn't enough air in the room to dispel the tightness in her chest. She had to change the subject, or she too would break down, but she had to be strong for the boy's sake. She pushed him away ever so gently and said lightly, "I think we did enough homework for today. Maybe we should upload another game.

What do you think?"

The days passed too quickly. There was no Eric. There was no Cindy. Roseann took to drawing the shades during the day and restraining William from going outside. They were spending all their time in the house, like fugitives, William doing his homework and watching television or playing video games. He stopped asking about his father and mother. Twice he wet his bed, and he started sucking his thumb.

Roseann was sure the neighbors were spying on her, peering through the slats in the blinds and slits in the curtains, lurking around her villa to catch William's shadow on the wall although, with the lights so low, the house existed in semidarkness.

Since it was important to make things seem as normal as possible, she accepted an invitation to go to a charity fundraising luncheon, planning to leave before the fashion show. Roseann had given Willian strict instructions not to answer the door or go outside. She didn't like to leave William alone, but she had to make things look as normal as possible, afraid her absence from community events would look suspicious. How long could she keep William hidden?

"I won't be far, just at the clubhouse. When I get back, I'll play scrabble with you."

William begged her not to go. He clung to her and tried blocking the door. "Stay, stay, Grandma. Don't go."

"I have to go. I promise, I'll be back as soon as I can. Now remember, do not go outside or peek through the windows." She hated reminding him to stay hidden, but what choice did she have? Roseann gave her grandson a quick hug and hurried out the door, her heart in her mouth. What if he didn't listen to her and he was discovered? What then? She really had to make plans for them to go home if she still hadn't heard from Eric or Cindy, which she doubted.

When she returned, she found William asleep on the floor in front of the door. She shook him gently. "Go to bed, sweetheart."

"Can I sleep with you?" he asked sleepily.

"Of course."

It was getting harder having William with her. She feared for his emotional health.

William sensed her anxiety. At night she heard him moan in his sleep, crying for Eric. "Daddy, Daddy." Slipping into the living room, she'd get into his bed and, hold him close, whisper that soon everything would be all right. But she didn't know what all right was anymore. She just knew that someone from the board was bound to confront her, and she must make plans to leave.

This time it was Susan who called. "Have you decided what you're going to do?"

"I'm going to sell the villa. I'm coming home with William."

"Maybe you should wait. Don't be too hasty. Things may get better."

"I can't stay here any longer. I'm coming home."

"In which case, we'll all help you. Count on us to be there when you need us."

Emotion clogged her throat. "Thank you. I love all of you."

There was no more talk of putting William in foster care.

"Have you told William you are taking him to Connecticut?" Susan asked.

"Not yet." Roseann's heart throbbed, anticipating the scene when she would have to tell William they were leaving. "I'm dreading telling him that his father is not coming for him. Oddly, he's stopped asking for Cindy."

"Kids are funny that way. He'll get over it."

"I doubt it," she muttered. *Even if he does, will I?*

When she clicked off the call, Roseann pressed her fingers into her temples and massaged the area on each side of her eyes. She'd had bad headaches before but never like this. Sometimes she saw double. *Am I getting migraines now?* she wondered.

William had been invited to be in the school play even though he was being homeschooled. He was to be a pioneer and Roseann outfitted him with a costume she made from clothing she found in a thrift shop. A brown plaid flannel shirt, a fringed leather vest that came down to his knees, and, of all the luck, a ratty racoon-tail she'd found in the dollar bin for a Davy Crockett hat. William was so excited to be in the play, enjoying the company of other children. What was there for him in an adult residential community? William did not belong here.

Roseann had gotten up extra early to drive him to the play rehearsal they were holding this morning. William was so excited about being in the play that he practiced his few lines over and over in the car on the way to school.

"I am a pioneer who came out West to farm my land and feed my family. We will grow corn, wheat, and potatoes so we have food for the hard winter ahead."

After dropping him at play rehearsal, Roseann stopped at the supermarket to buy the ingredients for dinner. William had been complaining of a toothache, so she reminded herself to make an appointment with the dentist before they left town. *So much to do.* She felt exhausted before she'd even started.

After arriving back at the condo and putting away the groceries, she still had an hour to spare before going back to school to pick him up.

I've got to start packing, she told herself. She took down her mother's gold-banded china. The service for eight was incomplete. Through the years, a cup, a saucer, a plate had broken. It was a discontinued pattern, and she hadn't been able to replace the pieces. But now the china was going to Connecticut with her. She paused and rubbed the edge of a saucer. It too was chipped. With trembling fingers, she wrapped each fragile piece of china in the *Sundial Acres News* and added it to the partitioned carton she'd brought back from the grocery store.

A new beginning.

The timer on the stove rang.

William would be waiting for her.

She must not be late.

CHAPTER SEVEN

Susan was finally getting to meet Gary Reingold in person. They'd met on a dating site, and it was apparent they had a lot in common. Initially they spent hours talking on the phone and texting each other. She was hoping Gary would ask her for a date. He said he wanted to see her, but he kept coming up with excuses for the delay. First, he had a wedding in Sicily; his cousin was getting married, and he said he was planning on touring Europe after the wedding. "Now that I have the time," he explained, "I want to go to all those places I always dreamed of seeing. I have an open ticket so I'm not in any hurry to get back."

"That sounds wonderful," she replied. "So you have no idea when you'll be back?"

"Not really."

"Well, enjoy yourself," she said, trying not to sound disappointed that he wasn't as anxious as she was to get together. Since she didn't hear from him while he was away, she thought this was his way of ending the relationship. She tried putting him out of her mind and was hopeful again when he called her when he got back from his travels, complaining about knee problems he'd incurred on the trip.

"I can hardly walk. It was all those hills and uneven sidewalks. I guess I overdid the hiking. I am not in as good shape as I thought." He laughed lightly. "According to my orthopedist," he continued, "I tore cartilage in my right knee. The pain is excruciating, as you can imagine, and I will need surgery to repair the damage."

"What a shame," Susan empathized. "When are you going for the operation?"

"The doc had a cancelation so fortunately he can get me in right away."

"Well, that is lucky," she said. "Sometimes you have to wait months."

"Of course, I will be out of commission afterward. It can take weeks until I am fully recovered."

"Knee surgery is not a walk in the park," she said, realizing later how stupid that sounded to someone who would be laid up with a bum knee.

"Sooo . . . I guess we will have to wait to meet up. But we can continue to talk on the phone and text," he suggested.

"Sure," she replied tonelessly, not expecting Gary would be calling or texting when he was so preoccupied with his knee problem. There would be more excuses. He would be having physical therapy and busy with follow-up doctor appointments. Maybe the whole thing with Gary was caput. *Nothing ventured, nothing gained,* she told herself. To her surprise and delight, she was wrong, because Gary called and texted and kept her apprised, in great detail, of his knee recovery. Now, almost three months after that initial contact, they were finally going to meet in person.

Susan had given herself an extra fifteen minutes to get to Armando's because she was hoping to see her date before he saw her. That way she could decide whether to stay or cut out. So many guys lied about themselves on their profiles—but the same could be said for the women. Her photo was at least five years old, and she was ten pounds thinner when it was taken. Susan studied the guy's photo from all angles, but it was hard to make judgments. He'd only posted one and it was grainy. Was his expression serious or mocking? Hard to tell.

When he called. she immediately liked his voice and the way he paused and didn't interrupt when she talked. They talked about a lot of stuff, mostly world events since there was so much going on and because they agreed on so many things—climate change, politics, books and movies they both enjoyed. When he finally suggested dinner, which seemed to take forever, she immediately suggested Armando's.

At Marlene's suggestion, the mah jongg group had gone there to celebrate Barbara's birthday even though Barbara had insisted there was no cause for celebration. "It's just another year."

"But we always celebrate each other's birthdays," Susan insisted.

"What a lovely idea." Grace flashed a smile at Marlene, knowing how difficult these past weeks had been for her taking care of her mother.

Marlene had raved about the food at the little local Italian restaurant. First, it was Al's favorite. Second, the portions were humongous, and third, Al said it was a good value.

Susan recalled that all four women had ordered the special, salmon over pasta. Armando, alerted to the occasion, had brought out a small cheesecake and four forks.

"Now make a wish," Marlene coaxed. Barbara closed her eyes and blew out the single candle.

When Susan told Marlene she had a date with Gary Rheingold, Marlene immediately asked if he was related to the beer family.

"I have no idea," Susan said.

"Do they still sell Rheingold?"

"I don't know. Maybe in some parts of the country. Ask Al."

"My Al's a Bud guy. You could google him and see if he's related."

"Honestly, I'm *not* that interested, Marl. But if it comes up, I'll ask him." Which wasn't quite true because Susan had spent a good deal of time googling Gary Rheingold. Other than some newspaper story about Harbor High's twenty-year class reunion, there was nothing but a blurry photo of graduates who attended the event. Gary could have been any one of the blazer-clad middle-aged men with their dorky smiles and balding pates.

"Make sure to call me when you get home," Marlene told her.

"Okay, okay," Susan replied, just to get the woman out of her hair. She hated being treated like some naïve teenager. Which she'd never been.

But Susan had to admit she was nervous about finally meeting Gary. To steady her nerves, she'd popped an extra Xanax before leaving the house, hoping it wouldn't make her loopy and dim-witted. Standing under the canopy outside Armando's, her heart was pounding and there was a tingling sensation in her legs.

When she'd left her house, it was drizzling. Now, blue-black clouds shrouded the sky. Needles of rain stabbed the asphalt. She'd parked her Lexus in the back lot, fought her umbrella. She tightened the ends of the magenta Hermès scarf wrapped around the collar of her three-quarter length Calvin Klein raincoat. Shivered. Under her raincoat she wore a scoop-necked cerise silk tunic and black stretch pants that hugged her hips.

It's ridiculous to wait outside just because I'm early.

A laughing, umbrella-less couple preceded her into the restaurant. The man, fiftyish, held the door for Susan then immediately turned back to the girl who looked half his age. Armando greeted the couple and ushered them to their table in the rear. While Susan waited, she tried to look nonchalant when Armando returned to the vestibule and flashed a toothy smile. "Table for one, signora?"

"No, table for two. My friend has not arrived yet. He will be asking for Susan. And, Armando, I would appreciate a table toward the rear of the restaurant."

"Very good, signora."

The table he led her to was, unfortunately, diagonally across from the couple she'd seen on her way in. She avoided looking their way.

"Would you like a glass of wine, signora, while you wait?"

"How is the house red?"

"We have an excellent burgundy."

She gave it some thought. A drink would certainly help steady her nerves, but she decided to wait. A drink might make the wrong impression. "Just some ice water with lemon. Not too much ice."

"Very good."

Susan hated waiting even though she had made sure she would be the one to arrive first. She examined her red manicured nails, picked the dripped wax on the Chianti bottle, studied the framed black-and-white photographs of the Colosseum, the Leaning Tower of Pisa, gondolas floating in the canals of Venice, and Saint Peter's Basilica on the wall. The décor was so tacky with the red-and-white-checkered tablecloths; she regretted choosing this place for their first date.

Her attention was first drawn to the couple across the way. The girl was laughing, throwing her head back as if whatever her date said was the funniest thing she'd ever heard. Next to them was an elderly couple who sat like statues. Their eyes stayed locked on their food until the woman turned to stare back at her. Susan quickly averted her eyes and pretended to have been looking at another table, where a husband and wife were seated with their little girl. The child looked around three years old, and Susan suddenly remembered one particular instance when she and Tony had taken Joy out to dinner when she was that age.

The memory was a splinter festering under a nail. Joy was generally a well-behaved child, but that day she'd gone to the doctor and gotten a shot and was running a slight fever. When the babysitter called and canceled, Susan wanted to stay home with the child, but Tony had insisted on taking Joy to the restaurant. Joy was cranky and the dinner was a disaster. She'd cried and cried, refusing to eat her food. Tony had immediately blamed Susan for Joy's bad behavior, calling her incompetent, and making such a fuss the people at the other tables turned to look at them. Susan wanted to crawl under the table with shame and embarrassment.

"You're too soft with the kid. What she needs is a little discipline." And with that he stood up, yanked Joy off her chair, and dragged her kicking and screaming out of the restaurant and made her sit in the car until she agreed to finish her food. When they came back, Joy picked up her fork and gagged. She threw up all over Susan's blouse, the imprint of Tony's hand on her red tear-stained cheek.

Thankfully, Susan was rid of the bastard. She'd been warned not to marry him. Her parents had been furious when she dropped out of college to be with an actor.

"He'll break your heart," her mother warned.

"He's got no future," her stepfather predicted. "Do you know how many actors actually make it?"

"I don't care," she cried. "I have faith in him. He's really good. He's already been in two movies."

"As an extra," her mother huffed. "Go back to school. Get your degree. At least that way you can get a good job because you are the one who will have to support the two of you."

"We're not going to give you one red cent," her father told her.

"I don't want your fuckin' money," Susan screamed, tears streaming down her face. "I don't want your help."

"You know it's all about sex," her mother warned. "That's all he cares about. It's all they ever care about in the beginning."

"Shut up. Shut the fuck up. I love him and Tony loves me."

She hadn't bothered to keep in touch after that. Her parents had turned their back on her when she ran away to marry Tony. She was too ashamed to admit they were right when Tony tired of her, even though the sex was damn good. Even when she became pregnant with Joy, she didn't call her parents. She knew he ran around with the students in his acting classes. He was always taking classes and did very little acting while she worked—part-time as a waitress, as a clerk in a bakery, and as a cashier in a supermarket—at anything she could get and still be there for Joy, who went to daycare. Her earnings barely covered childcare costs. Tony said he had to devote himself to improving his acting ability and refused to find part-time work that might interfere. So, it was up to her. Susan was exhausted both emotionally and physically. She had been glad when he left but was too proud to go back home.

When they finally separated, Tony moved to California and promptly forgot he had a daughter. Susan was thirty-two, a single mother with no money, no job, and no one to turn to. She raised Joy on her own. The best job she got was working at a spa at an exclusive golf club, thinking it was a good place to hook up with rich men. When she met Joseph Harris—he was twelve years older, married and divorced twice—she thought she had it all figured out. Marrying Joe was strictly for security. But as luck would have it, Joe had invested with Madoff and the marriage dissolved along with his investments.

The graceful house they'd lived in was mortgaged to the hilt. She had her jewelry and, fortunately, had been privately socking away money during the years they were married. Whatever was left had been whittled away. Susan had no job, no savings. But she had Joy, who she cherished. Joy was married and about to have a baby.

That makes me a grandmother. Don't frown, she told herself. *Worry lines make you look older.*

Susan was researching the number of calories in eggplant parmigiana versus chicken Francese on her mobile when Gary Rheingold suddenly appeared at the table.

"Susan?"

"Gary?" she said, startled. She half rose when he took the chair across from her and launched into an apology.

He was taller than his photo led her to believe, and his silver-streaked, sandy-brown hair receded over his high forehead, causing his face to appear leaner, his nose sharper, his eyes dark with light irises.

"Oh, I wasn't waiting long," she lied. "I actually just got here."

"Darn. There was so much traffic and the lot in the back was full, but I managed to pull into a spot right out front."

She hung on the word *darn*. "I . . . I only just got here myself," she repeated.

Armando was standing by the table. "I believe the lady was about to order a glass of wine."

Susan blushed. "Not really."

"Ah, in which case she shall wait no longer." Gary studied the wine list, his face full of consternation.

"Honestly, I can wait for dinner."

"But I would like a glass. Which do you prefer, white or red?"

"Armando suggested the house burgundy."

"We can do better than house." He ordered two glasses of sauvignon blanc, the most expensive choice—although there was nothing over thirty dollars—and sat back in his chair, hands nested in front of him on the table. She noticed his fingers were long, the nails short and evenly shaped.

After a brief recounting of the weather, the traffic, and the reason she'd chosen Armando's, including the successful mah jongg luncheon, Susan plunged ahead.

"How is your knee? I noticed you didn't have a cane."

"Thankfully, I'm fully recovered. It's amazing what doctors can do today. My knee feels absolutely perfect," he grinned, patted his leg.

A nasty thought flashed through her mind. Had Gary really had knee surgery, or had he made up an excuse to delay seeing her? Was there another woman in the background? She was being paranoid and quickly searched for another subject to ward off further suspicion. "You said in your profile you were retired. But in all the time we were texting and chatting you never told me what kind of work you did."

"It's no big secret," he answered. "It's not like I was in the Mafia. I managed a retail clothing shop for more than twenty years."

"Would I recognize the store? I love to shop." She laughed lightly. "I might have been one of your best customers. Is it local? The store?"

"No. It's in Westchester. The kind that sells preppy-type clothes. We're known for golf wear and school uniforms. Blazers, chinos. Where the cheapest tie for an adolescent boy is a hundred dollars."

"That is a bit steep. My daughter, Joy, she's a thrift-store shopper. And she always looks fabulous. Shabby chic. Not at all like her mom. I admit I am a bit label-conscious."

Susan could have bitten her tongue off. She must sound like all she did was shop. *Well, that isn't so far from the truth. He might as well be forewarned.*

"I think you look fabulous."

She lowered her gaze. "Why did you retire?"

"I don't miss the long hours or dealing with entitled customers, if that's what you mean."

"Mmm." She nodded. "I don't wonder."

"Besides which, retail is not what it used to be, not with the internet. I got out just in time."

Their appetizers arrived. They both had ordered Caesar salad, but Gary had substituted lemon and olive oil for the dressing. He took small bites, his pronounced Adams apple worked like a lever while he chewed. She watched, amused by his fastidiousness, how intent he was on his food, barely looking up while he ate.

"And what do you do?"

"My last job was office administrator in a medical practice," she offered, pushing her croutons and anchovies off to the side. "The doctor cut my hours when he changed his practice to concierge. I was downsized." She had improved on her story, not wanting to reveal the real reason she left, to the point where she almost believed her lies.

"Have you found anything else? Work, I mean."

"Not yet. I'm still looking." Another falsehood.

Which box would he check at the end of the evening?

Relationship possible:

a) Very likely
b) Somewhat likely
c) Unlikely

As for Susan, she was still trying to figure Gary Rheingold out when her cell tone alerted her to incoming calls. "Sorry, I meant to turn this off." Clicking the phone off, she put it in her handbag. *Marlene called twice, probably trying to set up this week's game even though she knows I'm on a date.*

Armando returned, asking if they would like to order another glass of wine.

"The sauvignon blanc was a little disappointing," Gary said. "Let me see the wine list again."

She kept quiet. She thought the wine was just fine.

While they waited for their main course, Susan took inventory.

For a man who was in retail, Gary could use some fashion advice. Tan corduroy sports jacket *(all he needs are patches on the elbows)* over a navy-plaid button-down shirt. She bet he was wearing cuffed kakis and Docksiders.

Gary raised an eyebrow. "Earth to Susan?"

"Sorry?"

"I asked if you enjoyed your chicken Francese?"

"Yes. What about your pasta? Did you enjoy it?"

"Yup. I have a weakness for pasta of any kind. Mine was delicious, but then I'm Italian. I can't go a day without pasta although it plays havoc with the waistline. My mother makes it every day."

"You're Italian. Really? Rheingold doesn't sound Italian." The comment about his mother intrigued her but she let it pass and made a more generic probe. "Tell me about your family. I wondered about your last name."

"There's not much to tell. My great-grandparents were from Sicily. Theresa and Mario Bonaventure, derived from Bonaventura, which means 'good fortune.' They had four sons, but three of them died, two from consumption and one was killed in the war. My grandfather, the youngest, came to the United States, but before he left, his mother went to the priest who told her she had to change his name because Bonaventura, good fortune, was tempting the devil."

"But how did he get to Rheingold?"

"My guess is he got this free calendar from Rheingold and just took the name." He grinned. "Gosh, there must've been some good-looking gals on the calendar, so he thought hell, why not."

Susan laughed. *Gosh*. When was the last time someone she knew said gosh? She rested her elbows on the table and propped her head on her hands, stared into his eyes, waiting for him to lower his gaze, but he did not waver.

"I like your laugh."

She felt the heat rise to her face. How should she reply, with "Aw, shucks"?

"Honestly, I don't have a clue how we got that last name. The funny thing is, Ma is a teetotaler. Won't touch a drop."

"Unlike the two of us." Susan lifted her glass so he could refill it. The wine was going to her head, and she did have that extra Xanax. Then, trying to sound neutral, "I was wondering if you were married or if there is someone in the picture." *Better to clear it up before things go too far.* "I told you I was married. Actually, I am twice divorced. Not proud of my track record, but life throws you curves."

"I'm not married. There were a couple of close calls. But no. Never married and no one currently in the picture."

"Hmm."

"Honest Abe." He raised his right arm, as if taking an oath for the Boys Scouts, and winked.

"And the reason, Mr. Rheingold, you are unattached?"

"I guess I'm still looking for the perfect person."

"Perfect! Perfect! Wow. That's a pretty tall order."

Armando reappeared at their table. "Have you had a chance to look at the dessert selections?"

"Give us a sec."

They both studied the dessert options.

"May I recommend the homemade cheesecake. Italian cheesecake made with ricotta. No calories if you share."

Susan was still pondering her date's excuse for being unattached. "Susan, are you okay with cheesecake?"

"Thanks, but I wouldn't know where to put it. Excuse me, but I think I'll visit the ladies. You can save me a bite, Gary."

Her balance was a bit shaky. She walked unsteadily, attributing her unsteadiness to too much wine and too many pills. When she came out of the stall, she checked herself in the mirror. Took out a comb and ran it through her hair. She'd just been to the salon and spent a bloody fortune to cover the interminable gray. Next, she reapplied her lipstick, taking great care not to go outside the lip line.

So, Gary had never gotten married because he hadn't found the *perfect* person. She was far from perfect. There was the tiniest zit on the side of her nose that the foundation had failed to hide. She had the urge to squeeze it.

Should she believe him? Perhaps there *had* been a perfect woman in his life, perhaps he had found her and lost her to some tragic accident, or she had run out on him trying to live up to his standards. She blotted her lips and threw the tissue in the waste bin. How many women had he pursued in his quest for perfection? How many women had he made promises to, made love to, put on trial, and rejected them in the end? How many broken hearts had he left in his wake? *Well, damn you Gary Rheingold, Bonaventura, Bonaventure, whatever; I am not perfect. You, sir, will have to take what you get.*

Susan returned to their table and forced a bright smile. She felt lightheaded.

"You okay?"

"Sure. I'm not used to eating so much. It was delicious. I'll take a taste of that cake."

Gary reached over and handed her a forkful.

"Yum." She licked her bottom lip.

He put his hand over hers. "Some more?"

"Oh, I couldn't."

She felt an immediate pressure between her thighs. The heat surging through her body was not menopause. She released his hand and took a sip of water to simmer the rising temperature that would be her undoing.

When the bill came, he took out his credit card.

"Thank you," she said huskily.

"Ready?"

Armando handed over her coat.

"I enjoyed dinner, Armando," Gary said. "Pasta almost as good as my mama's."

Again, the mention of mama.

"Thank you, sir. Come again."

Susan lifted her arms into the sleeves. She breathed in the telltale aroma of tomato sauce, not unpleasant, on his breath. Could you count tomato sauce as an aphrodisiac?

It was nine o'clock. They'd talked all through dinner, and all that texting and chatting, still what did she really know about him? Only that he liked to jog three miles a day, that he ate pasta that his mama made, that he was a retired retail store manager who dressed badly, that he used words like darn and gosh, and that he had absurdly high standards for women.

The rain was a lackadaisical drizzle. The streetlights glowed with a misted halo. They found her car and he held the door while she settled behind the wheel. She opened the window. The rain trickled onto her upturned face. "Good night. I had a lovely time."

"Me too." He bent down and their lips were so close they could have kissed. Her pulse quickened. He drew back. "You forgot something."

"I did? What?"

He handed her the closed umbrella through the window.

"Thanks. Hate to lose it. My best one," she said stupidly. "Well, I'd better get on my way. Thanks again."

"You're welcome. And Susan . . ."

"Yes." Her heart fluttered. "Always stay as sweet as you are."

Gary Rheingold turned and walked away.

Well, so much for Gary Rheingold, Susan muttered, offended by what was clearly a brush-off. *The man was perverse. Looking for the perfect woman. Bonaventura. Good fortune to you. Who did he think he was?*

Before she drove off, she checked her cell phone. In addition to the two calls from Marlene, there was one from Barbara. No messages. Strange. Barbara rarely called her unless it was to ask for a ride when her husband had the car or when Grace was unavailable to play. Something was up. She dialed Marlene's number.

"Marl, it's me. I saw you called."

Marlene's voice was breaking up. "I've been . . . try . . . trying to reach you. Why didn't you . . ." Marlene paused to sob. ". . . call me back?"

"You know I had a date. Marl. He's really something. And he's not related to the Rheingolds, for your information. Marlene? Marlene, did you hear me? What's wrong? Are you crying?"

"You . . . should . . . have returned . . ." She sobbed again. ". . . my call."

"My cell was off. What's wrong?" Marlene was gulping her words. It was difficult to understand her. "What's wrong, Marlene? Are you crying? Is it Al?"

"No, it's Roseann. She's in the hospital. They say she had a stroke. Susan, dear God, she may not pull through."

Her heart clutched. Roseann had a stroke. How bad was it? "Where's William?"

"He's with me. I don't know what to do."

"I'm coming right over. Marlene, hold yourself together. Is Al there?'

"He's putting William to bed. I don't know what to do. What if she . . . dies?"

"Pull yourself together, Marlene. It's going to be all right."

But was it?

CHAPTER EIGHT

The open house for real estate agents in her area was at ten. Barbara had scheduled a showing with an out-of-town client who was interested in buying a fixer-upper that already had two bids.

Hank was sleeping while she dressed in the dark, each movement measured so as not to disturb him. He had finally fallen asleep around two o'clock, two sleeping pills and God knows how many beers later.

She'd laid out her clothes the night before like a schoolgirl: a pair of black poly pants with a crease running down the center of each leg, a long-sleeve rayon blue-and-white striped blouse, black stacked heels recently resoled, and a tan blazer were the basics she counted on. The other brokers were always more fashionably dressed, but this was just an open house, and she had no idea whether this prospective client was worth getting more dressed up for.

Lucille and Myra, colleagues in her agency, leased expensive cars and could afford to take their clients out to fancy restaurants. They were married and, from what she could tell, their work was more like an avocation, something they did to keep busy, like weekly manicures, hours spent at the hair salon. Barbara didn't envy them for what they could afford, what she envied was their predictable lives with husbands who weren't in and out of work and who didn't wear them down the way Hank wore her down. She knew she should feel sorry for Hank. He was depressed and angry, but she was tired of being wife, mother, and cheerleader. She would like her husband to take more responsibility for his failures instead of laying the blame at everyone's feet but his own.

Very quietly, she opened the top dresser drawer and took out a vintage Hermès scarf. Without looking in the mirror over the dresser, she tied it loosely under the collar of her blazer. Scarves were her one extravagance. Thanks to Grace, who had introduced her to the Golden Purse consignment shop, she'd recently added a bit of panache to her otherwise staid outfits.

"It's a wonderful find," Grace agreed when Barbara showed her the pin she had found buried under an African beaded necklace in the showcase. It was in the shape of a violin. She held the pin up for Grace to see the backing. "See? It's marked silver. And those are tiny diamond chips. I'm almost positive."

Grace laughed. "So buy it, for heaven's sake. You won't starve! You can raise my rent!"

The pin was an extravagance with Hank out of work, but she decided to splurge for its inherent sentimental value. It reminded her of her mother who never showed her disappointment in her daughter's lack of musical ability. Her mother had played the violin in the local orchestra. She was an accomplished musician who was unable to further her life's ambition to play in a national orchestra. When her mother wasn't busy taking care of Barbara and her two younger brothers, she'd take a few moments to practice. Barbara loved listening to her. It still amazed her that her mother had managed to carve out time to do the thing she loved most in the little free time she had. Selling real estate was definitely not Barbara's passion. But what was, she did not know and didn't have time to think about.

Starting at an early age, Barbara went to all her mother's concerts. After the performance, her mother would introduce her to the other musicians who made a great fuss over the little girl, a miniature version of the petite attractive blonde with the shy smile, blue-violet eyes, and faraway lost-in-her-own-world expression when she picked up her bow.

"What instrument are you going to play?" the musicians would ask Barbara. Oh, but little Barbara was hopeless as far as music was concerned. She loved to listen to music—classical, modern, jazz, country—and liked nothing better than to put one of her mother's vinyl records on the record player and pretend she was playing in the orchestra or band. Sadly, Barbara discovered she was tone-deaf, like her father. Try as she would, and she did try—the piano, the flute, even the drums—she simply didn't have the talent for playing an instrument. She was too spirited and impatient to harness her energy and exercise the patience she needed to play an instrument proficiently. She was more suited to sports like gymnastics, where she excelled.

Barbara's father had no real appreciation for music, and she often wondered if her father's inability to share his wife's passion was the reason their marriage broke up. Her parents divorced when she was ten. Since her mother and father never remarried and lived nearby, Barbara wasn't one of those children who felt abandoned by one or the other. She'd had a separate relationship with each one, so they remained a part of her life until they passed. The time they were a family, living under the same roof, was a shadow in her childhood. She had loved each equally and never blamed them for going their own way.

When she showed the pin to Hank, his response was, "You wasted your money. It's silver plate, not sterling, and those so-called diamonds are glass."

Of course, she was hurt by his criticism, but she tried not to show it. Hank, she knew, was in one of his moods. What was the point of arguing? The woman at the shop had assured her the pin was authentic sterling silver and the diamonds were real and good quality, a unique piece from an estate of Victorian jewelry from a prominent family. Besides, even if she had been "taken," Barbara was delighted to have the pin and glad Grace had encouraged her to buy it.

This morning, she pinned it to the lapel of her blazer and fingered the shape lovingly, wishing things were easier. She looked back at Hank, who'd thrown the covers off and was sleeping with his arms flung across the bed.

She recalled Grace buying silver hoop earrings that day; the earrings were the size of bangle bracelets, and they swayed back and forth when she moved her head to show them off. Her smile was wide and her eyes mischievous. "What do you think?"

"They're perfect," she recalled complimenting the earrings that she thought were a bit over the top. "I could never wear anything like that, but on you they look great, really."

Most of the time Barbara looked forward to going to the open houses when the brokers got together to assess a property that was newly listed. But today she was going to have to pretend that all was right with the world when she was reluctant to leave Hank alone. She decided to stop by the cottage and ask Grace to talk to Hank. She had recently read an article about vocational testing, and it had occurred to her that this was something that could help him. The battery of tests was designed to align skills and interests with different fields of work. Hank had many skills that could be applied to a variety of jobs, except he didn't know where those skills fit.

Grace must know all about this, she thought. Maybe Grace could convince Hank to take these tests. It was worth a shot.

Barbara was afraid to get her hopes up, but she decided she would stop by the cottage and ask Grace what she knew about this vocational testing. Maybe Grace could even give him the tests.

One more time, Barbara looked over at her husband. His breathing was ragged. Morning peeked in between the drawn drapes and lit up one side of his face. He was even more handsome asleep. Her heart went out to him.

She continued dressing for work in the dark, feeling her way around the room, carefully putting away her nightgown in the bureau and opening the closet to find her shoes. She was exhausted. He'd kept her awake with his tossing and turning. She had finally gone to the living room and slept badly on the couch.

Soundlessly, she closed the bedroom door and went into the bathroom to brush her teeth and put on her makeup. Sighing, she appraised herself in the mirror. The foundation and concealer had failed to cover the dark circles under her eyes. The nub of Cherries in the Snow lipstick accentuated the fine lines around her mouth. She darkened her eyelashes with mascara and rubbed pink blush on her cheeks. She ran a wide comb through her hair, careful not to tug the strands. A month ago, she had gone to the dermatologist, concerned about the bare patches on her scalp.

"My hair is falling out," she had cried.

"It's all stress related. It's a condition called *telogen effluvium*; the thinning is probably temporary. Is there anything specifically that might be causing you stress?" the doctor had asked.

"My husband lost his job. He keeps losing his job and I'm worried about him. He's very depressed." She hadn't added that he was taking it out on her. "Also, he's drinking too much."

The doctor had pressed her lips together, adding to her notes and then writing a prescription. Her voice was sober. "You have a lot to contend with. I'm quite sure when things get back to normal, your hair will grow back."

Back to normal. Barbara frowned, applying a topcoat of lip gloss. *What the hell is normal?*

Finally, she was dressed, ready to leave. She stood on the porch. Daylight beamed and the morning sky was threaded with long wispy cirrus clouds. She hesitated then walked the short distance to the cottage next door. Her heels squished in the dew glistening on the grass.

CHAPTER NINE

Grace was not that surprised when Barbara knocked on her door. She'd had a feeling Barbara would be coming to see her. Last night she had watched Hank pacing outside and heard Barbara shouting for him to come in. The lights in their bedroom window shone brightly when she finally fell asleep around twelve thirty. Her nighttime and daydreams were filled with thoughts of Hank and Barbara more often than she liked.

"Sorry to bother you. I know it's early," Barbara apologized.

"Oh, I've been up for hours," Grace said. "I was just about to have some herbal tea. Would you like a cup?"

"I have an open house at ten."

Grace tightened the cord around her bathrobe and stepped aside. "Is everything okay, Barb? If it's about the leaky faucet, I was able to get a washer at Jake's Hardware, and I can change it myself, so there's no need to get a plumber."

"No. That's not . . . not it." Barbara stammered. "It's Hank. You must have heard him last night."

The woman was shivering. "Well, don't just stand there. Come in."

Barbara followed Grace into the kitchen. Even though it was early, the kitchen was immaculate. Not a thing out of place. The tea canister and sugar bowl were in the center of the table alongside a plate of toast and jar of English marmalade.

Barbara hadn't been inside the cottage for a while. She hated to be one of those nosy landlords always checking on a tenant. But there was no need since Grace was the perfect tenant. Her rent was paid on time; she even took care of the outside chores, mowing the lawn and weeding the vegetable bed without being asked, painting and repairing what needed attention on the inside of the cottage. She had refreshed the original dark-stained wooden kitchen cabinets with a creamy coat of paint and changed the rusty hardware so the new brass shone. She had replaced the dingy gray tile with black-and-white checkerboard squares. Plants flourished on the windowsill. Barbara couldn't help but admire the new look. She wished she could do a similar makeover in her kitchen, but Hank would not want the inconvenience and they couldn't afford to hire someone to do the renovations. Of course, Hank had enough time on his hands to do the work himself, but Barbara was not about to suggest that.

Sitting at Grace's kitchen table, taking in all the improvements, she wondered if Grace was bothered sufficiently by Hank's erratic behavior to be thinking about moving. Grace had never commented on his raucous drinking bouts, his flare-ups. But then, if anyone could understand Hank's behavior, it would be Grace. She wouldn't worry about the possibility of Grace moving. There was enough on her plate to worry about.

"The place looks wonderful. Are those new?" Barbara pointed to some ceramic plates on a shelf above the stove. "They look Mexican."

"Oh, those. I picked them up at a flea market last weekend. Also, that brown pottery jug with the flowers. There's a crack on the back you can hardly see. I was able to patch the crack with Elmer's, so hopefully it won't leak." She took it off the shelf and showed Barbara where she had mended the jug.

"The woman who sold it said the jug was quite old; possibly a hundred years although I think that's a stretch. I'm not sure of the marking. I should probably look it up."

"Or take it to that show on TV."

"*Antiques Roadshow?*"

"Yeah and find out it's worth a million bucks."

"From your mouth to God's ears." Grace refilled her cup with hot water and swirled the original teabag. Reaching across the table, she placed her hand on her friend and landlord's clenched fingers. Her touch was warm and comforting. "Barbara, I have the feeling you didn't come here to talk about my bargain hunting. What's bothering you, dear?"

The air hinted of some lavender cleansing detergent, light and fragrant. Morning sunlight skimmed through the lace tie-back café curtains. Barbara swallowed the lump in her throat. "Grace, I have a favor to ask you. I really didn't want to . . . maybe I shouldn't have come here."

Grace was used to clients not being able to come right out with what was bothering them, so she smiled her engaging smile and encouraged Barbara to continue. "Is it about Hank? He was pretty upset. I saw him last night. He spent a long time outside, walking back and forth. Shouting. He'd obviously been drinking."

"That's why I decided to come see you. Hank lost his job again. And he's drinking too much. I thought if you could talk to him about going for some counseling . . . both for the job issues and to cut back on his drinking."

Grace knew Barbara was going to be disappointed by what she had to say. But she had no choice. It was better to be honest than set false expectations. She took a deep breath. "You know, Barbara, I would like to help, but I'm too close to the situation. There are boundaries. His . . . Hank's issues are . . . complicated. He needs someone who can be objective, and I'm afraid that's not me. No, please let me explain. The problems around work, I might be able to recommend someone I work with. A voc counselor. As for the drinking, there is AA."

"I know Hank won't talk to just anyone. But he *will* talk to you. You are a voc counselor, aren't you?"

Grace got up and replaced the jug on the shelf to give herself time to think, while Barbara glanced at the clock on the wall that always read eleven thirty.

The clock had been in the cottage when Grace moved in. It had belonged to Barbara's grandparents, and Barbara kept it as a way of remembering the good times they'd spent together, she'd explained when Barbara took Grace around the cottage, and they decided what she should keep and what she could give away.

"I don't mind if you replace it with something digital," she'd told Grace. "You don't really need a clock. You could just use your phone or iPad. Honestly, you don't need that old thing. I'll have Hank take if off the wall."

"But it was your grandparents," Grace had protested. "I wouldn't think of taking it down."

That was Grace. She kept it because she knew how much the clock meant to Barbara. Barbara loved Grace, who was so thoughtful, so understanding. Why would she refuse her request now?

Barbara waited. Finally, Grace said, "I can't get involved, Barbara. I'm sorry. The thing is, I'm too close to the situation. I would like to help, but I can't."

"But Hank trusts you."

"Oh, Barbara. I'm not sure he does." Grace hated to hurt Barbara. If only she would see it her way. To understand the dilemma. "There are professional boundaries. Barbara, I'm your friend, your tenant. Hank is your husband—"

"Yes, he's my husband," Barbara repeated dully. "But he's not the man I married. Hank's lost . . . he's angry. He frightens me with his tirades. I'm afraid of him." There, she'd said it.

Grace sat up straighter. She stared at Barbara. What had she missed? Were there signs of physical abuse? There were no black-and-blue marks on her face, but she was wearing a lot of makeup. Grace tensed. Her heart was pounding. But she had to know. "Barbara, has Hank hurt you, abused you physically? You can tell me if you need help."

"No. Hank has never laid a hand on me. It's true that he forgets himself sometimes."

Grace was not convinced Barbara was telling the truth. If Barbara was going to confess that she was being physically abused, *sometimes he forgets himself*, it was best she came forward on her own accord. If it was true, Barbara was not ready to tell her.

"What then, Barbara? What is bothering you?"

"It's not me I'm worried about." Barbara squeezed her eyes shut as if the thought was too terrible to contemplate. "I'm afraid Hank is so unhappy, so desperate, he might hurt himself."

"Do you have any reason to suspect he is planning to hurt himself?"

"No. But the possibility of suicide terrifies me. How could I live with that?"

Grace pushed her cup aside, tea splashing on the Formica tabletop. She blotted the spill with a paper napkin. She knew she was being manipulated, but what could she do? "What you're asking, it's not right."

"What do you mean, it's not right?"

"I'm too involved. I'm too close to the situation," she repeated.

"But that's the point." Barbara leaned forward. "It's better that you're the one who is involved. You know Hank, the real Hank. It's not like he's some stranger you don't care about. You have a relationship. You're my friend and you understand what I'm going through. What he's going through. You understand his suffering."

"Grace, think about it. That's all I ask."

"I don't know, Barbara."

"I have that open house at ten, and then I'm meeting a client. Promise me you will stop by the house and talk to Hank. Make up some excuse." She was begging. Had she no shame?

"I can't make any promises."

"Then you'll talk to him."

Grace nodded. She felt trapped. "I'll need some excuse why I'm stopping by. I'll think of something." The fact was she didn't want to see Hank alone. Not that she was afraid of him. Quite the contrary. He reminded her of some of her male clients. Under that cockiness, that anger, there was a needy person waiting to be saved. And there was no denying he was good-looking.

"I know you will."

"The best I can do is to try to convince him to go to an AA meeting."

"And you'll tell him about the voc counseling."

"Yes."

Barbara stood up and straightened her blazer. She fingered the pin on the lapel. The tails of one of the new scarves she had wrapped around the collar of her blazer brushed her cheek. She was flooded with relief. "I knew I could count on you, Grace. I'll stop by later today and you can tell me how it went."

Barbara left the cottage feeling lighter. She could sense the change. It was called hope. Frail as a thread. But it was there. Except she had unloaded her burden on Grace who did not want to see Hank, who had once come on to her. Hank, whom she did not trust.

CHAPTER TEN

At ten thirty, Grace knocked on the door. She waited, half hoping Hank wouldn't answer. But he came to the door, still partly asleep. His hair was longer now, and a shock fell over his forehead as he recognized Grace standing on the threshold.

Grace had not seen him this close up in a while since the incident when he came on to her. Yet she was happy to see him. HIs beard was stubbled like rough sandpaper and the smell of alcohol and pot clung to his clothes. How many days had he been wearing that torn sweatshirt? It was clear he was decompensating, not taking care of himself. Depression did that to a person. She had seen that happen to many of her clients and it saddened her to see it in Hank.

There was an awkward moment of silence while Grace tried to find her voice and Hank tugged at the top of his sweatpants seated below his waist, exposing a narrow band of pale skin and a pencil line of hair down his stomach.

"Barbara's not here. What do you want?" he growled, his elbows crossed over his chest.

"I thought I would get her mah jongg set. I'm having the game this week and Barbara said I could borrow it."

"Shit, you came for that? She could've brought the fuckin' thing over."

"Sorry. I wasn't thinking. Of course, you're right. I could have waited until Tuesday's game."

"Damn right. Do you know where she keeps it?"

"Maybe in the hall closet?"

"Maybe in the hall closet?" he mocked her. "Well, go on and have a look."

Her instinct was to go back to the cottage, tell him she'd come back another time. But she'd promised Barbara she'd have this talk. Damn her.

Grace waited for Hank to step aside. When he did, he inadvertently brushed her shoulder. The sensation sent a faint tremor through her body. She followed him into the hallway. Grace was tall. But the closet shelf was high up, and she stood on tippytoes to reach beyond the jumble of hats, scarves, and shoeboxes to search for the mah jongg set. When she reported, "Not there," he challenged her with an amused glint in his eyes.

"You sure about that?" He reached over and brushed her hair with his fingertips.

She pushed him back when she stepped away. "I didn't see the case. Never mind, it doesn't matter. I'll tell her I couldn't find it. She may keep it somewhere else."

"Yeah, right. Come off it, Grace. You didn't really come for the fuckin' mah jongg set. Did you?"

Grace's cheeks burned. How obvious was this ploy? How stupid of her to use this lame excuse. He saw right through her. Of course, he would.

"No, I didn't come for the mah jongg set," she admitted. "Barbara stopped by this morning. I didn't want to come here, but she is very worried about you."

"Oh, really?"

"She asked me to stop by. To see how you're doing after last night."

"She did that? My poor frightened wife. Came to you, complaining. Huh. What about last night?"

"I heard, well, I saw you outside last night. You were in pretty bad shape. Barbara told me you lost your job and that you were very depressed . . . and she wondered if my talking to you would help. She thought since I work as a voc counselor, maybe I had some suggestions how you could find work."

He shook his head side to side. "Really? My very *concerned* wife is arranging a therapy session with our tenant, who turns out to be a voc counselor. How thoughtful."

"It's not meant to be a therapy session. She thought some casual conversation, where I would tell you about these tests people take when looking to change careers. It might be something you'd want to know about."

He laughed a false laugh. "Change careers. Oh, really? Do you know what Barbara wants me to do? She's hinted that I work for her brother, who has a plumbing supply business. My dear thoughtful, very concerned wife wants me to sell toilets and sinks. Did she happen to mention that career change?"

Grace raised an eyebrow. "She didn't mention that, Hank."

He snorted. "Oh, no, well now that you have that piece of information, what is there to talk about?"

"Look, I didn't come here to pressure you into going into a family business. I came over because your wife is also worried about your drinking."

"And the bitch wouldn't let you off the hook. Am I right? And that's the only reason you're here."

Grace sighed. "I said I would come over because Barbara is my friend and you both happen to be my landlords. I wasn't happy about doing this. I told her there was a problem crossing boundaries. Anyway, like I said, talking to you about going for voc counseling and seeing someone about your drinking problem is not therapy, Hank. It's just talk. I'm offering some advice you can take or leave."

Hank hit the coat closet door with his fist. "Talk, talk. That's all it is. So start talking."

His outburst startled her. Grace tried to keep her voice level while her heart was palpating. "How about you forget I stopped by. I'm sorry I interfered. This is between you and Barbara. I better leave."

"That's your call."

When she tugged the door open, a cold blast of air rushed in.

Hank grabbed her arm. His grip was tight.

"Hank," she winced. "Let me go."

"Calm the fuck down. Look, you're here. You might as well stay." He started walking down the hall to the kitchen. Without thinking, she followed him.

"Sit down," he commanded. "I'll make some coffee."

The kitchen was dark with the slats of the metal blinds closed. She felt trapped like some nervous animal. She felt the pulse in her throat throb. What was she doing staying here? "Hank, I really need to go."

"Sit down." Hank pointed to the chair opposite him. She did as she was told. "So tell me, Grace, do you like living in the cottage? Watching me from your window? Or were you standing on your porch to get a better view of me last night?"

"Could you please turn on the light? I don't like sitting in the dark."

"Afraid of the dark are you, a big important social worker like you."

Grace got up and switched on the light. She felt better with the lights on. She watched him go to the sink and refill the teakettle with water. Her head said *leave*, but her heart said *stay*.

"Barbara said you fixed up the cottage."

"It's my home now. I wanted to make it cheerful."

"So, you plan on staying then?"

Her antenna was up. Where was this leading? "I would like to. Why do you ask?"

"Barbara is over the moon you're next door."

"I'm glad it's working out. I really like your wife."

"And what about me? Do you really like me?"

"I do when you're not . . . you know. When you're more yourself. I heard you last night when you were walking outside and yelling at somebody. Naturally, I was concerned."

"Naturally. Ha. I saw you watching me. I knew you were there. I like you watching me."

She folded her hands in her lap and intertwined her fingers. She bit her lips afraid to say anything. *Yes, she did like watching him.*

"Do I make you nervous?"

"Not really." Her denial was caught in her throat.

"You know what?"

"What?"

"I think you're attracted to me and that's the real reason you came over."

"Look, Hank, I don't know what you're getting at, but the only reason I came over is because Barbara asked me to. She asked me to talk to you about getting some help for your drinking and to suggest meeting a vocational counselor. Taking a battery of tests. That's the *only* reason I am here, so don't make this out to be more than it is."

"So how about I talk to you? Right now? You're a shrink, right?"

"I'm a clinical social worker. I work at a social service agency, and I am planning on opening a private practice. I specialize in addiction issues, and I have done vocational counseling at the agency. But I am not prepared to take you on as a client . . . for obvious reasons. Those being, as I said before, my close ties to you and Barbara. It's not professional."

"So let's start talking. Where do you want to begin? With my childhood shit?" He turned on the burner and then sat down at the table, reaching for the butt of a cigarette he'd left smoldering on the chipped saucer already overflowing with butts.

She noticed his nails were bitten to the quick, the cuticles raw and red-rimmed. The tips of his right thumb and forefinger were stained the color of piss. He took a new cigarette out of the pack and lit it with the smoldering butt stub, inhaled, sucked the smoke deep into his lungs, and let out a stream in her direction.

Grace coughed, pushed the saucer that served as his ashtray to the farthest end of the table.

"You want some coffee? Instant?"

"No, thanks. But you go ahead."

He didn't make a move to get up. Grace shrank into herself while

Hank narrowed his eyes that traveled over her body like a slow waterfall.

He blew a stream of smoke across the table. She covered her mouth and nose. "I really wish you'd put that out."

"You afraid you'll get cancer? Secondary smoke?"

There were cartons of empty beer cans by the garbage pail. Ignoring his jab, she asked, "So exactly how much do you drink? I imagine you do pot and coke. How often? if I may be so bold."

"Whoa, girl. What's with the interrogation? And *exactly* what are you trying to get at?"

"If I am going to refer you for counseling, I need to get some idea of the extent of your problem."

Hank snickered. "Me, I don't have a problem. The only problem I have right now is getting you to fuck me."

Grace pushed away from the table. The surface was greasy. She reached for a crumpled napkin, thought better of picking it up, and wiped her fingers on her skirt. "I better go. There are lots of competent therapists I can recommend. I'll text you and Barbara their contact information."

"Grace, you just don't get it, do you?"

"Oh, I get it all right. I heard you. And I'll tell you right now that's not going to happen. Hank, you don't need to fuck me, you need to get on with your life. Barbara wants her husband back. As for me, I don't want to get involved. You need to see someone and face your problems."

He leaned forward and pointed his finger at her. "You think some shrink who'll give me some fuckin' pills, talk me through hell and back is going to help me get on with my fuckin' life?"

"Maybe, maybe not. But it's better than the life you have now." She started toward the door. "Honestly, I don't know why I listened to Barbara. I knew this wasn't going to work. Tell her I was here. Tell her whatever you want . . . You better turn off the stove. The water's boiling."

"You're done here?"

"There's no point staying." Why was she tearing up? Why was her heart breaking for him? She knew better than this. She had to, must leave. Now.

"Grace! Wait," Hank said, crossing over to her.

"What's the point?" she repeated, tearfully.

"Stay. I want you here. Please, don't go. Not yet." He wiped her cheek with one finger, then pulled her into him.

"Stop. What are you doing? Please don't," she sobbed.

"It's okay," he murmured. "It's okay."

She pressed closer into him. He smelled rank but she didn't want to pull away. *It's wrong, all wrong.* She burrowed her face in his neck. When he ran his fingers through the labyrinth of black springy tendrils, she knew she was lost.

He lifted her head. Kissed her eyes. Her mouth. Kept on kissing her. She gasped for air and managed, "Please, Hank, this isn't what either of us wants."

"I don't believe you know what you want, Grace. That's your problem," he murmured lifting her blouse and cupping her breasts.

It was true. This was what she wanted. She wasn't going to fight him.

It was only the sound of the front door opening and the voice reaching where they clung to each other that drove them apart. They froze, then stepped away from each other. Grace smoothed her blouse and licked her lips, erasing any evidence of what had just transpired. But she couldn't still her frantic heart.

"Hank, I'm home. My client canceled and the rest of my day was kind of slow, so I thought maybe we could go out for lunch—that is if you're up to it."

Barbara stepped into the kitchen. Momentarily stunned by the two people staring back at her, only then did she realize who they were. "Grace, I'm so glad you stopped to talk to Hank after all. Thank you. Hank, Grace wasn't sure, but she said she would think about it. How did it go?"

Flustered, Grace said, "I follow . . . followed your advice, thought I would take a stab at talking to Hank. That's what we were doing when you came home. We didn't expect you until later."

"I know, but that client, well I told you all that. And what did you two decide?"

"Hank agreed to go for counseling. I made him promise he'd also go to an AA meeting. They hold one at Your Lady of the Apostle Church on Wednesdays. You can check the schedule on Google."

"That's wonderful. Hank, you will go, won't you?"

Hank nodded. "She sure has a way about her. I guess so."

"Grace, you are amazing. Thank you. Will you go to lunch with us?"

"Can't. I'm meeting a client. I better go now."

"Well then. See you at mah jongg Tuesday? Oh, and you don't have to host the game. Marlene said she would have it at her house. Al has some kind of board meeting. What's this?" Barbara bent down and picked up a shiny object off the carpet. "I think this is your earring, Grace."

CHAPTER ELEVEN

Susan, Grace, and Barbara were sitting around Marlene's kitchen table. It was Tuesday, but no one touched the jumbled tiles on the card table. They were talking in hushed voices, but it was not because Al objected to their being here.

"How long has he been here?" Barbara asked, referring to William who was not within earshot but downstairs in Al's man cave playing video games.

"We took him in when Rosie went to the hospital," Marlene replied over the yelps and mild cursing that rose from below. Al and William were plugged into *Super Speeder*, a deadly car-crashing video game Al had streamed onto his humongous TV.

Al had neglected to shut the door to the basement. The women could hear the two shouting from below.

"Got another one!" William yelled when his neon-orange car careened into Al's car, flattening the blue speedster against a barricade like a tin can, "Ha. You're dead meat, Uncle Al."

"Not till the fat lady sings, son." Al's black speedster miraculously overtook the orange car at a record-breaking three hundred miles an hour, sending sparks into the air as it burst into flames before reaching the finish line.

"Shit!" Al let out without thinking. "Sorry, William."

"That's okay, Uncle Al. How about we play *Dino Beasts* next? Can you download it?"

"Sure thing."

Soon sonic blasts from dinosaurs with bat-like wings and feathers launching into space rang out. William aimed his virtual bow and an arrow plunged into the primordial beast's leathery breast. The dino howled a bloodcurdling cry.

Susan jumped. "Isn't that noise driving you nuts?"

Marlene got up and went into the hallway and closed the door to the basement that Al had inadvertently left ajar. When she returned to the game she said, "Sorry. They're just having a good time. Al's as hooked on these adventure games as William. He missed his board meeting at the firehouse just to be with William."

"Poor child must be traumatized. First his father dumps him at his grandmother's and then Roseann had that stroke," Barbara said.

"He doesn't sound traumatized to me." Susan winced because the pounding was coming up through the floorboards.

"It's amazing how resilient kids are," Grace declared.

"I wish Hank had some of that resiliency," Barbara uttered under her breath, but Grace heard her and gulped. She was still guilt-ridden about that episode with Hank that Barbara had failed to bring it up. She wished she would. It would melt the frost that was building up between them.

"What does Roseann's doctor say? Will there be any permanent damage?" asked Susan.

"Thank God, the stroke was not as bad as we thought."

"Well, you sure frightened the crap out of me, Marlene. When you called me, you made it seem as if Roseann was ready for last rites."

"Sorry. I guess I overreacted. I tend to do that."

"It's perfectly understandable. I mean you were the one who found her. Good heavens, it's very lucky you used your head and got her to the ER in time," Grace ventured.

"I only did what any one of you would have done in that situation."

"Oh, Lord," Susan thought. Let that not be a signal for Marlene to reenact her experience rushing in to save her dearest friend. Grace had primed the women that it was important for Marlene to describe what happened. "It's a kind of PTSD. We really need to be patient and listen."

Just then Susan's cell pinged. *Gary.* "Sorry ladies, but I've got to take this," she said as she escaped into the living room to take the call while the other women sat back and pretended no interest.

Marlene began, "It was Friday, and I was on my way to Costco. I generally don't go on Friday because it's so crowded and finding a parking space near the store is next to impossible. But I was planning on making a standing rib roast. We were expecting some of Al's Rotary buddies and their wives for Saturday dinner, and you can't beat Costco's prices. Since Rosie and I share a membership, I thought I would ask her if she wanted to split the paper towels and toilet paper. I mean there are just so many rolls of paper towels and toilet paper a person can use."

"Very sensible. That's something you and I should think about, Grace," Barbara said.

Grace replied, "Well, maybe." The last thing she needed was a half dozen rolls of toilet paper if she was planning to move.

"I rang the bell I don't know how many times and, when there was no answer, I got this feeling in the pit in my stomach that something was wrong."

"I would have thought she was just out with William," Barbara said.

"Roseann won't admit it, but she's hard of hearing. I have been telling her for months to have her hearing tested. You ever notice how she's always asking us to repeat a discard?" Barbara said.

"Maybe they should have done that while she was in the hospital," Marlene mused.

Susan returned in time to hear Marlene's suggestion. "I doubt they test hearing in the neurology unit." She was pissed. Gary had called to tell her he was going to be out of town for his cousin's daughter's wedding in Chicago and that he wouldn't be seeing her this weekend. More family weddings, she groaned. There was a rash of them. Why had he waited until now to tell her about a wedding invitation he must have gotten weeks ago? Was this some made-up excuse not to see her? Was there someone else? She sighed. She was being paranoid again, untrusting. Gary didn't owe her anything, she reminded herself. She hadn't even slept with the guy and here she was doubting his commitment. Well, that was about to change, she vowed. The next time she saw Gary, sex was on her agenda. Definitely.

Marlene was going into greater detail. "I found the key that Roseann hides under the ceramic flowerpot on her porch."

"That's the first place a burglar would look. It's like wrapping your money in aluminum foil and putting it in the freezer thinking they'd never find it," Susan noted.

"Talk about cold cash," Grace quipped.

"My mother hid her diamond earrings and her engagement ring in the ice maker." Barbara laughed. "She was upset because the robber took the ice trays too."

"But go on, Marlene. You were saying?" Grace encouraged.

"I found the key and let myself in. William was watching TV, and Rosie was lying on her recliner. When I asked, 'Rosie, why didn't you open the door?' she just stared at me like I was a stranger. 'Rosie, are you okay?' I shouted. Still no answer. I just knew something wasn't right. 'William, how long has your grandma been sitting like this?' I asked, and he said that his grandmother always falls asleep in front of the TV if she doesn't like the program.

"I got really nervous, and I told William he had to pack some things because his grandmother needed to go to the hospital. He argued that he wasn't going anywhere, and I'm afraid I lost it at that point, which I shouldn't have, and I said, 'William, you will do exactly what I tell you to do!' and said he wasn't to talk back. Next, I called Al, and it was lucky that I got him because he was about to go to the gym. I told Al about Rosie, and he said I should ask her what her name is and how old she is, and did she know where she lived and . . ." Marlene began to sob. "And she couldn't or wouldn't answer me. And I just knew it was awful. That she might die if I didn't get her to the hospital in time."

Susan raised her hands above her head. "And hallelujah! Here comes Al to the rescue. Just like *Grey's Anatomy*."

Grace patted Marlene's hand and glared at Susan, who had decided to text Gary and tell him about her disappointment then changed her mind and deleted what she'd written.

"My Al was amazing. He rushed right over and administered oxygen or whatever it is he does in these cases. I was busy helping William pack, trying to comfort him. Al drove Roseann to St. Ann's and because he knows all the nurses in the ER, they took her right away. If it hadn't been for Al, she might have waited Lord knows how long for the police to come, and they might have left her on a gurney in the hallway."

"You did the right thing, Marlene, to call your husband," Grace reassured her. "That way you lost no time getting help for Roseann. You stayed calm. You took care of William."

"Ladies," Susan interrupted, "I think we should get back to the issue at hand. How we can help Roseann when she comes home. It is going to be difficult for her to care for William. We need to stay focused. How can each of us help her?"

"I still say we should try to contact Eric. He is Roseann's son and William's father, after all, and he has a right to know what's going om," Barbara maintained.

"I don't think he has any rights after what he did, dropping him off like a FedEx package," Susan retorted, her arms crossed over her chest and glaring at Barbara who, she felt, was the most insensitive person she'd ever met.

Marlene agreed they should wait before contacting Eric. "Maybe it would be better if we could find William's mother first."

"Cindy? That bitch! I don't think that would improve matters," Susan said. "She never even tried to contact the child all the time he was in Florida with his grandmother. Even now, where is she? What kind of mother is she?"

Grace waited for the air to cool before offering her advice.

"I just worry that William will have to go into foster care," Marlene said. "We don't want to get social services involved if we can avoid it."

"I agree. Even disabled, Roseann is better than that good-for-nothing son of hers and that Cindy," Susan declared. "Let's not contact the parents. William should be our responsibility until Roseann can take care of him."

Grace wasn't sure if social services would approve of them not getting in touch with William's parents, but she said nothing. It was true that the boy seemed perfectly happy being with Marlene and Al. As for his going into foster care, oh, she knew all about that, having witnessed enough sad scenarios in her years working with displaced children in care.

"When do you think Roseann will be able to come home?" Barbara asked Susan.

"The last time I visited her in the hospital I got to talk to her doctor who had stopped in to see how Roseann was doing. He said Rosie is ready for rehab. It will take a lot of physical therapy, but he is optimistic she will regain use of her right arm and leg."

"How long will she be in rehab?" Grace asked.

"Anywhere from three to six weeks. It all depends on her progress. It's hard to tell right now. But that's why I called us all together. I think we should discuss how we can help her when she comes home after rehab," Susan reminded the women, who tended to go off track.

The women turned to Marlene, expecting her to offer to keep William.

Grace sensed Marlene wanted to say something but was reluctant to admit how she felt. "Right now Marlene and Al have opened their home and their hearts to the boy. But the full burden can't be theirs alone. You are doing a great job, you and Al, but it's only right we do our part. Don't you agree, ladies?"

Grace smiled appreciatively at Marlene who glowed with the compliment.

"What can we do?" Barbara asked.

"We could take turns with the driving and the chores. Set up a kind of schedule so we know who's available when and what we are each willing to do," Grace went on.

"That's what I was thinking when I called us together. It was not just to play mah jongg," Susan said, "although we could do that later if that noise settles down," wincing at the booming that managed to break through the barriers.

"The poor kid is going to feel like a bouncing ball if we take turns, never knowing who to expect or if we are going to show up," Barbara argued. "I think he is best off being here with Marlene and Al. He's used to their routine."

"But we will have a routine once we know who has agreed to do whatever needs doing," Susan responded.

Marlene frowned. "I hate to have to agree with Susan. Al and I have a life, Barbara. And with Mom being sick, I am already in overload."

"William won't feel like a bouncing ball. Not if we have the right attitude and we present this as a positive," Grace insisted.

"I bet he was used to being shuttled around by babysitters and neighbors when he was living with his mother and then with his father when his parents separated so it shouldn't seem that odd to be with so many 'aunts,'" said Marlene.

"William really misses his grandmother. He's accepted that she's sick and needs to stay in the hospital to get better and I've explained about her going to rehab before she's allowed to come home. He's talked to her on Zoom while she was in the hospital since he couldn't visit her. He said she looks and talks funny. I think he's worried what it will be like when she comes home." Susan then proceeded to tell the women about the conversations she'd had with William about what he could expect. She even acted out their conversations to the delight of her listeners:

"'How will she look different, Aunt Susan? Will her arm be in a cast? Last year Peter Sullivan in my class broke his arm playing soccer and we all signed our names on his cast.'"

"'No, William, her arm is not broken, the muscles are weak, but they will get stronger and that her face might look kind of droopy.'"

"'Like she tripped and fell and broke her jaw? That happened to this kid I know who has to eat baby food.'"

The women laughed in spite of themselves.

"Go on," Marlene urged. "This is hilarious."

"I said that it might be a little difficult for Roseann to walk without a cane. That didn't seem to bother him. He said he thought his grandmother talked kind of mushy and that it was hard to understand her. 'That will get better too,' I told him. When I told him that Roseann was working with a speech therapist, he said, 'They got a speech therapist in school for kids who stutter.'"

"Does he understand that his grandmother had a stroke?"

"That was really funny. He said, 'How can grandma have a strike? She never plays baseball. She won't even pitch balls to me when I want to practice my batting.'"

The women nearly fell off their chairs laughing, picturing Roseann in a baseball uniform with a glove and a bat.

"I tried to explain what a stroke was. I said it's when the brain gets a blood clot and there is a lack of oxygen when I realized I was getting far too technical, so I stopped myself and told him to go look it up on the internet. To go see Dr. Google and type in what is a stroke? He is a whiz at the computer."

"Brilliant," Marlene clapped her hands.

"And then what?" Grace prompted.

"I assured William we would all be there to help him and his grandmother. That when she got out of rehab we would be taking turns to make sure he got to school on time and to his activities. He wasn't sure why she was in rehab. He said his father was in rehab and I had to explain the difference. That was tough."

"I can imagine," said Grace. "Poor kid."

"How did you explain the difference?" asked Barbara.

"I said this kind of rehab was like a gym when they teach people how to use the body parts that don't work so well anymore, and that his grandmother was going to get much better at walking and talking and all that. I didn't go into the other rehab. And he didn't ask, thank goodness."

"You did a fine job. Couldn't have done it better myself." Grace gave her a thumbs up.

"Now to get back to what we are going to do," Susan said. "We all know that Roseann is going to need a lot of help and is too stubborn to ask for it. The doctor said Rosie was not to exert herself, which means no driving, no housecleaning, no grocery shopping, no cooking meals, and no just about anything, which is going to be very difficult for someone like Roseann who is a take-charge person."

"I talked to Marlene earlier and we agreed that we should all chip in and get a home health aide to stay with her the first couple of weeks," Grace reported.

"Of course, she says she doesn't want a home health aide living with her," Marlene added. "She thinks she'll be able to do everything herself once she's finished rehab and comes home."

"Do you have any idea how much a home health aide costs?" Barbara cut in. "I have enough on my plate right now without paying for a live-in, so you can just count me out."

Susan ignored Barbara for the moment. "Can we please get back to William? We still need to sort that out. We haven't discussed what each of us is willing to do."

"Ahem. Excuse me, ladies. Sorry to interrupt." Al stood in the doorway.

"What is it Al? Can't you see we're busy?" Marlene snapped.

"Got any more chips, Marl? And we could use something cold to drink. How about you rustle up a couple of sandwiches? William is getting hungry. Boy, can that kid eat."

"Why don't you order a pizza and have it delivered, Al. I'm talking to the girls. We're trying to figure out a schedule for when Rosie comes home."

"Pizza. Good idea. Okay, ladies. Hope the noise isn't too much for you."

Susan turned to Marlene when Al left the kitchen to return to the basement. "You're right. Al has really taken to the boy."

"William is a sweetheart, and I wouldn't mind keeping him, but he belongs with his grandmother. Do you know what he said to Al when Al explained why it was taking this long for his grandmother to come home. He said, 'When my grandma comes home to get better, I'm gonna take care of her. I'm gonna carry her packages from the supermarket and carry the laundry down to the basement.'"

"What a love," Grace gushed.

"The boy belongs with his grandmother, even if it is going to be difficult for her. That's why we need to set up a schedule," Susan reminded them.

"I absolutely agree that we should keep things as normal as possible," Marlene said. "Al and I can alternate driving him to school and picking him up. We are doing that now."

"And I can take Monday afternoons, seeing how it's the slowest day to take clients house hunting," Barbara offered. "Broker open houses are on Mondays, but they are usually in the morning when William is at school. I can do some grocery shopping, and I'll be responsible for Monday meals. It's just he can't stay at my house."

"That's terrific, Barbara. You do what you can." Grace turned to Susan who said,

"I can do Wednesdays. That advanced yoga class is too difficult, so I don't mind switching to the Thursday moderate class. My manicures are Fridays, and massages are Mondays, so Monday wouldn't work for me anyway. I never know about Fridays. As for meals, unless Roseann objects, there are awfully good restaurants that offer takeout. Count on me for Wednesdays."

"I think William has swim class on Wednesdays. I'll have to ask Roseann for his after-school activity schedule. And Susan . . ." Susan had tuned out; she was checking her phone. *Damn. Why hasn't he answered me?*

Grace tried to bring her back to the conversation. "Susan, I think takeout would be a nice treat."

"What about Thursdays?" Marlene asked.

"I'll talk to my clients and see what I can rearrange. I work at the clinic on Mondays, so I'm glad Barbara is up for Monday. I could probably drive him to school some days. I have to check my calendar." Grace carried a thin black appointment book that was a freebie from her dentist. The printed agenda was a backup to her digital scheduling app. In the event her phone crashed, she wanted to know she had hard copy. "Yup. I'll do Thursday. I think we haven't covered Tuesday or Friday yet. Barb, Susan?"

Susan made a wry face. "I guess I could take Fridays since my boyfriend is always busy on Fridays."

"I can do Tuesday, so long as my sister is willing to pitch in with Mom. Hmm. I guess I could take William to the hospital and have him wait in the family room . . ."

Grace nixed the suggestion. "Oh, that wouldn't be a good idea, Marlene. He's seen enough of hospitals. Maybe your Al could help in a pinch."

"Of course." Marlene spoke over the raucous whoops thundering from Al's man cave. "I'm sure he won't mind some more play dates."

The women laughed.

"As for the weekends. I guess it will have to be hit-and-miss for each of us. But we should check in with each other, so we know who's available when. I'm sure we can work this out."

And they did stick to their schedule with very little confusion except for the time Susan was supposed to take William to a last-minute soccer practice that interfered with her massage appointment.

"I couldn't very well cancel," she explained. "That appointment cost me three hundred dollars without the tip. I was lucky to get Marcel, the head masseuse. He's always booked way in advance."

"But what about William and his soccer practice? Wasn't he upset to miss it?" Barbara asked.

Susan lowered her eyes admitting to the women that William had indeed missed his practice. "He got a kid's massage instead. Gratis. And he *loved* it."

CHAPTER TWELVE

William had no problem with the mah jongg ladies taking charge of him. In fact he liked all the attention he was getting, On the days he stayed with Aunt Susan, they did arts and crafts. He'd drawn a picture of his grandma with some crayons Susan found in her junk drawer that were too old to be any good, but he used them anyway, He struggled to outline the features of the portrait. The picture was to be Roseann's belated birthday present since he didn't get to spend it with her when she was in the hospital. She was too sick to have a real birthday cake Aunt Susan explained, so they celebrated it on Zoom. But now he could go to the rehab center since she was feeling much better.

Roseann was excited to finally see William. She got dressed in the new pants and blouse Susan had bought her, and even put on some makeup.

William waited while Aunt Susan was talking on her mobile, telling the person on the other end that she wasn't sure she was up to seeing him this Saturday, but maybe Friday.

"What's wrong with Fridays?" she asked. And when she got off the phone, she seemed really angry because she yelled, "He thinks *I* should be more understanding."

Adults have all these weird ideas. William stared at his portrait of his grandmother. It sorta looked like her, he thought. She'd like it, even if it was a little smudged where he'd tried to fix the eyebrows that looked like upside-down Vs.

When Aunt Susan came back into the room, she told William to hurry up and get dressed. He was already dressed but she made him change his T-shirt. This was the one his father had bought him when he took him to a Mets spring training game in Clover Park, Florida. He tried not to think about his father too often because it made him so sad.

"It's time to visit your grandmother." She sounded a bit mean. Then, just as suddenly, Aunt Susan took a deep breath and said she was sorry if she was a bit harsh. "But that man is maddening," by way of no explanation. William had no idea what she was talking about. His stomach was growling. Aunt Susan didn't keep any good snacks that he could just help himself like at Aunt Marlene's. He decided to ask if there was enough time for him to have a peanut-butter sandwich.

"Of course. I forgot all about lunch. I am so sorry, William. I'll make you a sandwich, and how about a hot chocolate to go with it?"

"That's okay, Aunt Susan. But I did notice you have a can of Coke in the refrigerator."

Susan grinned. "Sure," she said, thinking, *like that bastard I'm dating, you've got me over a barrel.*

"We better get going. Your grandma is expecting us, and we don't want to be late."

William focused on the strangeness of the neighborhood they were driving through to get to the rehab clinic. The buildings were taller than the ones where Grandma had her house, and there was a serious feeling about the white brick building and the black-and-yellow directional signs with words he could not make out—*ambulatory, maternity pavilion, rehabilitation.*

"Now, William," Susan began, leaving her car at the valet entrance, depositing her keys with the guard, and side-stepping a man in a wheelchair buried up to his neck in a plaid blanket. "I already told you that Grandma may look a little different when you see her. And you are not to tire her out by talking too much." Susan tightened her grip on the boy's small hand that felt even smaller in the cavernous reception area as they made their way to the bank of elevators.

"I won't," he said warily.

They walked down a long corridor that smelled of antiseptic and boiled cabbage. Susan wrinkled her nose and tried to pretend that everything was perfectly normal. But it was far from normal, and she worried about William and what he might say to Roseann when he saw her.

"Room 105. This is it," she said relieved to find Roseann sitting erect in an armchair rather than slumped in the wheelchair.

"William," Roseann cried. "William, oh, William. Come here and let me see you. I think you grew three inches since I last saw you."

Shyly William walked over to the chair. "Hi, Grandma," he said. "I promise not to talk too much."

"Don be shilly. You talk as mush ash you want."

That was the signal and William chatted away. While her blue eyes did not sparkle, the laugh lines still turned up at the corners of Roseann's mouth when he entertained her with the silly jokes and riddles he saved like coins in his piggy bank to buy presents for his mom's and dad's birthdays. Her laughter, though smudgy, rang out. Grandma Roseann was his best audience.

"I have a new riddle, Grandma. What is brown and sits on a piano?"

"I don know. Wha?"

"Beethoven's movement."

"Oh, thash a funny one."

William frowned. "Who is Beethoven, Grandma?"

Susan and Roseann laughed.

"A famish composher," Roseann replied.

"Oh. What is a composher?"

Susan and Roseann laughed again. Roseann even elbowed Susan in the ribs to show how much she was enjoying their company, but she was growing tired. Susan hadn't told her what the mah jongg group had planned for when she came home.

"William," she said, "why don't you go out in the hallway and find a nurse. Ask her if she has any milk and cookies for you. I think they keep snacks in a little kitchen. And you can get some juice for Grandma."

"Okay," William replied. He was growing hungry and also a little bored. He wished they had video games he could play, but all there was was a television in Grandma's room, and Grandma said it wasn't working.

Susan pulled her straight back chair next to Roseann's. She took Roseann's hand and began, "The mah jongg group met last week and we talked about arrangements for when you get home," she began.

"Wha kinda arrangements? I don need any help." Roseann said, suddenly alert.

"You are going to need help around the house, making meals, taking William to his appointments. That kind of thing. We want to make things as easy as possible for you."

"I don't wanna health aide if tha's what you're thinkin'."

"We know that. That's why the women are going to take turns driving William to school, doing the grocery shopping and bringing you meals. It's just until you can manage all that yourself."

Roseann slumped in her chair. Susan reach behind her and adjusted her pillow.

"Now you wouldn't mind us doing that, would you?"

"I guess not," Roseann said wearily." Where's William?"

"He went to get a snack."

There was a long pause while Roseann took a moment to close her eyes.

"Oh, here's William now."

Roseann tried to sit up straighter. She adjusted her weak arm so it rested in her lap.

"Here grandma. I got you some apple juice."

"Thank you. I wash thirshty. Here you open it and I'll drink it later."

Susan got up from her chair. "William, we mustn't tire Grandma out. Roseann, we will come again," she said, signaling to William that it was time to go. "Say goodbye to your grandma, William."

"Bye Grandma."

"Tell her you love her."

"I love you, Grandma."

Roseann's head had fallen to her chest. Soft birdlike noises whistled through her lips. Susan put her arm around William and together they left the room, waited for the elevator that was clogged with other visitors who got off at different floors.

"I am very proud of you," Susan said when the valet driver brought the car around. "You made your grandmother very happy."

"I am very sad," William said when he settled in the passenger seat and Susan drove away.

"Why, William. Grandma was so glad to see you."

"But I forgot to give her my drawing."

"You'll give it to her the next time we visit. And for being such a good boy, I have a special treat." Susan found her purse and handed him the package of gummy bears she'd bought in anticipation of the visit. "And you don't have to share them, not unless you want to."

CHAPTER THIRTEEN

Five weeks later Susan and William arrived at the rehab center to take Roseann home. Roseann had packed her small suitcase filled with the greeting cards she'd received and the clothes she'd worn during her stay. She had also saved the small soaps and hand sanitizers she'd not used. Susan carried the suitcase and a plant that was a gift from the mah jongg women to the car and put the collapsed wheelchair and cane in the trunk.

Roseann was settled in the front and William in the back. He waited until there was a backup of traffic and found the drawing he had made for his grandmother. Leaning over the front of Roseann's seat, he dropped the gift wrapped in leftover Christmas paper he had secured with lots of scotch tape in her lap.

"What is thish?"

"It's your birthday present. I'm sorry it's so late, Grandma. I kept forgetting to give it to you."

"Ish never too late to get a preshent." Roseann tried unwrapping the gift, but her fingers wouldn't work.

"Let me," William offered. "There's a lot of Scotch tape." He leaned over and took the gift back.

Susan yelped. "William, what the hell are you doing? We are going to get into an accident. Sit down."

William ignored her and dropped the present back in Roseann's lap.

Roseann gasped when she saw the portrait William had made

of her. "Thish ish the besht birtshday preschent I ever got." Spittle puddled around her mouth while she extolled the colors of the sky, the birds, the sun, and the clouds like the diadem for a Madonna that bore a very slight resemblance to herself in her grandson's eyes.

"I sorta messed up," William said. "That's because the crayons were crappy, so I couldn't get a good point."

Roseann's laughter was a more like a turkey gurgle rising from the back of her throat. She brought the drawing closer to observe the writing.

Get Wel Grandma. From William

"Oh, I think ish fine the way it ish. I absholutely do." Roseann did her best to work her mouth in an upturned U. She held out her left arm with the drawing. "Here, Aunt Sushan, you shave it and make sure it doeshn't get creashed."

She reached for her tote bag and put the picture away. "I am going to have it framed. That way you can hang it on the wall and admire it while you're getting better."

"I would like that very mush."

While they drove, Roseann opened and closed the fingers of her left hand. All week she'd been exercising the fingers with a ball that reminded her of the pink rubber Spaldeen she'd had as a child. She forced her fingers to rhythmically squeeze and release, squeeze and release, squeeze and release. She looked at the fingers—like dead fat wrinkly worms that were of absolutely no use.

She used to be proud of her hands, the long straight fingers and almond-shaped nails. Now the fingers were riddled with arthritis. Her knuckles were gnarled, and her wedding band dug into her flesh. It used to slide on and off easily when she washed her hands. Would they cut the ring off when they buried her? But no! She mustn't think about death. Not while she was responsible for William. Now that she was going home.

Susan was exhausted from driving into New York, weaving in and out of traffic and getting stuck behind aggressive cab drivers who cut her off when she shifted lanes. Most of the time she took the New Haven line, preferring sitting and reading to fighting city crazies who hogged the road. What she needed was a glass of wine and a hot bath. She was also exhausted from all the chatter. William went on and on about all the things he had done this week. The karate lessons and the special news that the teacher said he could keep the hamster for the weekend. "Would that be okay?" he asked shouting over the traffic blare. "I promised the teacher I'd clean the cage every day, so it doesn't get smelly."

"William," Susan snapped. "Your grandma has enough on her plate without a hamster in the mix."

"Oh, I think we can managish for a few daysh."

When they got to Roseann's apartment, Susan settled Roseann her in the living room on the new black leather recliner she'd had delivered as a welcome home gift, and called Marlene and Grace to make sure they were stopping by later to bring dinner. Grace said she would pick up a few things at the supermarket for breakfast. Barbara was scheduled for the weekly shopping. Roseann was to write a list, using the pen with her left hand. She never used the shopping app on her phone, even before the stroke.

"I don't know how to thank you all of you." When Roseann learned what the ladies were planning, tears welled in her eyes. "I've been so mush trouble. Sush a nuishance."

William interrupted Susan, who was telling Roseann she was anything but a nuisance.

"Can I, can I stay over Aunt Marlene's tonight?"

"Instead of being with your grandma?" Susan cocked an eyebrow. "But you just got here, and Grandma will need you to do things for her. And you are supposed to take care of the hamster, remember?"

Roseann yawned. "If thash what you want, you can go." She closed her eyes.

The doctor had warned her to take it easy and to pay better attention to any signs of trouble. Dizziness, weakness, headaches, loss of vision, confusion—the very symptoms she had ignored the day of William's class play.

"What you had at the time," the doctor said, "was a mild stroke. It was a warning for what you suffered this time. You were very lucky. I don't have to tell you." He was about forty, Eric's age. Roseann brushed the thought from her mind. Wasn't Eric the one she had to thank for the situation she was in? The stress she was unable to manage, the anger she was unable swallow?

Roseann was courteous. She wanted to reply that no one had to remind her that it was a blessed miracle she was here or forewarn her that the next time she might not survive or become more of a vegetable than she already felt she was. *I know, I know. Take more medicines, stick to a better diet, and exercise three times a week.*

Roseann thought back on all this and leaned back, her head falling to one side as Susan looked at the latest text from Gary. Yes, he wanted very much to see her. They needed to talk. About what? She wondered. The next text was from Marlene. Of course she could bring William back to the house, but who would stay with Roseann?

Susan decided it was better to call Marlene, rather than keep texting, but Marlene didn't answer her call.

"I'm going to call Grace," she said aloud. "Maybe she will be available tonight to stay over."

"You know," Grace said when Susan explained the situation, "I've been rethinking; we should get someone to be with Roseann the next couple of days. Just until we're sure she can manage on her own. I'd feel a lot better with someone in the house all the time and not us just dropping by."

"She is entitled to a visiting nurse, and William is here," Susan said. "Except he wants to be with Marlene and Al tonight." She glanced at William who fidgeted with the hamster cage, trying to unlock the door so he could refill the water tube.

"William is just a boy," Grace replied. "That's asking a lot of an eight-year-old."

Roseann shook herself awake. Even though she was only able to make out one side of the conversation, she knew that Susan and Grace were adamant about hiring a home health aide. "I'm shi . . . shine," she stammered. "I don want a shade."

William looked at his grandmother. Aunt Susan was right. Grandma was his responsibility. He felt much older than his years. He stood up and threw his shoulders back. "I changed my mind," he said stoutly. "I want to stay with my grandma. I'm not like my dad; I don't run away when I'm needed. And my grandmother, she needs me. Right, Grandma?"

"Yesh my prechous. I need you very mush."

CHAPTER FOURTEEN

Al had just dropped William off at school. As a reward for doing so well in school, he promised to take the boy to an indoor golf driving range. "The kid is a natural," he was telling Marlene. "You should see him swing."

Marlene was unloading the dishwasher while Al finished his late breakfast of scrambled egg whites and unbuttered whole wheat toast. Since his last visit to the cardiologist, Marlene was taking seriously the warning that Al's blood pressure was dangerously high. His cholesterol level had also elevated since his last physical. She monitored his food intake like a boot camp sergeant, limiting his salt intake and thinking she could get away with veggie concoctions when what he craved was a juicy steak and cheeseburger.

This morning she was banging the dishes and slamming cabinet doors and drawers, ignoring her husband's complaint that Dr. Rodham didn't know what he was talking about; anyone could just look at Al and see he was in great shape for his age.

"I'm canceling that follow-up appointment," he said.

Marlene heaved a deep sigh. "I don't care what you do," and then she surprised herself and Al by sobbing. "All you think about is yourself when you know what I'm up against."

That stopped Al in his tracks. He got up and put his arms around her shaking shoulders. "Oh, I'm sorry, baby. I forgot. I really did. Today is the day you're meeting your mother for lunch to go over her eulogy, isn't it?"

"Yes," she quavered. "I'm sup . . . supposed to pick her up and we're going to that awful Chinese restaurant she likes." She picked up the dish towel and swiped her runny nose.

"The one Bonnie used to say that smothers everything in—"

"Ubiquitous brown sauce," Marlene finished. In spite of herself, she laughed. Her daughter hated having to eat there when she visited her grandmother, but it was her mother's favorite restaurant and neither Marlene nor Bonnie had the heart to tell her what they thought of the food.

The day before, her mother had called and asked Marlene to take her out for lunch. "I want you to go over my eulogy. I have it written out and you can read it when we meet for lunch. I want you to tell me if it sounds okay."

Marlene was speechless. *Your eulogy and you want me to tell you if it sounds okay?*

"Marlene, did you hear me?"

"Yes," she gulped her reply. "When do you want to meet?"

"Tuesday. Pick me up around noon."

"Does it have to be Tuesday?"

"I have doctors' appointments Monday and Wednesday. Wednesday, I get another infusion and I'll be exhausted and in no mood to eat."

Tuesday was mah jongg but to reschedule their lunch so she could play was selfish, so she agreed to meet her mother Tuesday and forego the game. Susan was understanding. "Of course," she said. "No prob. I'll call the others and see if we can find another day that works."

But finding an alternate day was not easy. Roseann was not sure she was available to play. She said she was finding it hard to focus on the card. The last time they had gotten together, Roseann was apologetic. "I don wan to shold up the shame."

"Don't you worry about holding us up, Rosie," Marlene had said, smiling at her friend who was doing remarkably well, considering. "Susan does that all the time and she hasn't had a stroke."

Susan had stuck out her tongue. "Very funny, Marl."

Barbara said she wasn't able to come up with another day, not giving a reason. Then Grace had begged off, explaining she had clients coming for couples counseling. But they had already cancelled two other appointments, so she wasn't sure.

Before hanging up with Marlene, Susan expressed her frustration with trying to organize the mah jongg game. "There's something not right between Barbara and Grace. Have you noticed?"

"To be honest, I haven't been paying attention. I have too much on my mind to worry about the two of them."

"I get it," Susan said. "I just thought I'd mention it. Is everything okay, Marl?"

"It's just having lunch with my mom." She broke off, not wanting to go into detail about the reason for the lunch. She was still grappling with how she was going to handle the situation. It was unfair of her mother to ask her to comment on her eulogy. What was she supposed to do if it was awful? Or soppy and unclear?

"You take care of you," Susan said. "And don't worry about the girls. They understand what you're going through."

That Tuesday, Al offered to drive Marlene to her parents' house. It was kind of him to offer, she said, but she'd rather he didn't come, knowing how much Al and her father disliked each other. "You'll be stuck keeping him company and that won't be pleasant for either one of you. I'll need you to pick up William and give him dinner."

"Of course. Don't worry about a thing. William and I will be fine. Give your father my regards. Maybe I'll get me and your dad a couple of tickets to go to the fights at the Garden. I know how he likes to watch them on TV. Take his mind off your mom."

Al's devotion to William, his eagerness to help Roseann, and now his change of attitude toward her father was surprising. Al hated the fights and the fact that he was offering to take her father was a real peace offering. She was so proud of her husband, observing this softer side she knew he had but didn't often show.

By the time Marlene crossed the Throgs Neck Bridge, she had gathered enough courage to tell her mother she couldn't read her eulogy, let alone make any corrections. The idea was absurd and unfair.

But her nerves failed her by the time she stopped at the pharmacy to pick up her mother's prescription. On a whim, she bought three chocolate bars and ate one while driving through the neighborhood that still felt like home despite her abandonment and the many changes: the three-story high school that replaced the one she'd gone to, a box food mart that took up an entire block, a triplex movie theater, two drive-up banks, and a Burger King and MacDonald's, each with a kiddy playground.

She pulled into the narrow driveway that separated her parents' house from what used to be the McCains's before Mr. McCains died and his wife moved in with her son and daughter-in-law in one of the Carolinas. "Poor thing lives above the garage like a recluse" was how her mother had described her friend's living arrangement.

Marlene always got a bit nostalgic whenever she visited her parents. This was the house where she'd spent most of her childhood and teenage years when her parents moved from the Bronx and bought a house in Queens. She was only twenty when she left to marry Al. For the first year, they lived a couple of miles away from her parents. When they moved to Connecticut, it felt as if she were moving to another country and deserting her mother, who made no bones about mourning her absence.

Marlene sighed when she looked around. Death loomed inside the small ranch house but had not touched the exterior. Tangled forsythias, sticks when they moved in, were bursting with buds. The daffodils had tripled, boldly yellow; pink and purple hyacinths spiked the loam. Johnny jack-ups with their unabashed faces had reseeded in the vacant flower boxes.

Her mother was standing behind the storm door watching out for her. She was bundled in a winter coat, a knitted hat pulled low over her ears despite the spring-like weather. She opened the door and took the brown paper bag.

"It's twelve thirty and you were supposed to be here at twelve. What's this? We're going out to eat."

Marlene said too brightly, "I got your medicine and some dark chocolate bars. Dark chocolate is rich in flavonoids; it's an antioxidant and supposedly good for the heart."

Her mother scowled. "A bit late for that, isn't it?" and went into the kitchen to fill a glass with water.

Marlene followed the animated voice of a sportscaster into the living room where her father reclined on an Easy Boy (one of the few new pieces of furniture her parents had bought since she left home) facing the TV. It was the season's opening game at Yankee Stadium and the Mets were up against Chicago.

"Who's ahead, Pop?"

"The Cubs are creaming them." Her father waved her away from blocking the screen. "She's been waiting all day."

"I'm taking her to Chang's." Usually, it was to the doctor or food shopping. Her mother was no longer up to going to the mall.

"I don't know how anyone eats that crap."

"Well, she likes it, and she needs to eat. She looks terrible. She's down to nothing."

Her mother was never really fat, more on the pudgy side. When Marlene looked at her parents' old photographs, she could see what must have attracted her father because her mother might not have been beautiful, but she was damn sexy looking.

One day her aunt told her, "Your father was quite the Don Juan. He attracted a lot of women, and the women loved him. Then he met your mother and they fell in love. The problem is your mother loved your father more than he loved her. The real story, I suppose, is my brother; he ruined both their lives when he seduced her, and she became pregnant. Those days, he was forced to marry her. Funny thing is she lost the baby. Course they were already married, and your father was stuck with her."

"I didn't know that, but I sensed there had to be something that was wrong between them. There was this bitterness, this chasm. For a long time, I wondered why they stayed together if they weren't happy."

"People of my generation didn't get divorced. Not like today. You just stuck it out."

How much was there about her parents she didn't know? She reasoned that her mother was either protecting Marlene or was too ashamed to admit what had happened to her. Her mother was so naïve at the time she'd met her Romeo. What did her mother—or girls back then in general—know about sex, about protection? They didn't have the pill, that's for certain. Who did she have to enlighten her about contraception?

Marlene wished her mother had been more forthright about her marriage to her father. If only she knew, she might have suggested her mother seek therapy rather than harbor all that resentment (and take it out on her kids.) Ha. Her mother would never go to a psychologist. Even now, knowing she had cancer, she believed you just deal with what God hands out. What was her favorite saying? Man makes plans and God laughs. Well, Marlene wasn't laughing now. Her heart was breaking thinking about their lunch and what her mother expected her to do.

She sat on the couch and waited for her mother who, when she came back, stood in the hallway and called, "Okay. Let's go." She did not acknowledge her husband when she slammed the door. Marlene bent down and kissed the top of her father's balding head. She felt the need to apologize to her father as if she and her mother were engaged in a conspiracy. Did he know her mother had written her eulogy and asked her to edit it? Marlene had always oscillated between love and despair regarding her parents. She had hoped her mother's illness would draw them closer, but it was only the anticipation of her death that interested him.

Marlene didn't think she could face her father after such an emotional lunch. Before she left, she said, "I'd stop back after lunch only I promised Al I'd be home by four."

Her father grunted, swiveled the recliner away from her. "Do what you want."

The only other people in the restaurant were retirees. Chang's was a foregone conclusion—the furnishings were bone-tired: hobbled mismatched chairs, chipped cups and saucers, tea-stained tablecloths, menus flecked with bits of food. The dusty brown carpet was threadbare at the entranceway. She could taste the peanut oil and fishy soy sauce with each breath. They selected a booth toward the rear. It was eerily dark for daytime, and her mother had an even more ghostly pallor. Above their table, the blades of a ceiling fan wafted faded crepe-paper streamers and frayed tinsel festooning Chinese New Year lanterns. Somewhere a fluorescent light flickered and buzz-buzzed like a wasp.

Marlene noticed the healthy choices—steamed broccoli, bean sprouts, bamboo shoots and cloud-ear mushrooms—were all à la carte. When the waiter came over, she took her cue from her mother and selected a combination plate from the luncheon specials.

She managed to steer the conversation away from the eulogy—Cousin Elaine's pregnancy and a friend's acrimonious divorce. By the time the waiter arrived with their bowls of egg drop soup, her mother had cornered her by handing her a pink paper torn from her personal writing pad (*From the Desk of Mildred Weisman*) with her typed eulogy.

"You need to tell me what you think."

"This is very difficult."

"I know. I wouldn't have asked, but I need an outside opinion."

Marlene flinched as if she'd been slapped, "An outside opinion? I'm your daughter."

"Sorry. What I meant was . . . just read it and tell me if it's clear. I need to know."

There was an awkward pause while Marlene read what her mother had written. She nibbled her lower lip, took a deep breath, and said, "The eulogy is perfectly clear. It says everything that must be in your heart."

Her mother broke out in a smile. Relief flooded her face. "You really think so?"

"Yes. Yes, I do."

"I wasn't sure when I put it down."

Marlene was still reeling from having to give her mother her opinion. "Of course, it's hard to be objective about someone's eulogy, especially when that someone is your mother."

Her mother said, "Thank you for doing this."

"You're welcome. You don't have a thing to worry about." This was the closest she could come to honesty. It was a repeat of the past with Marlene saying what she knew her mother wanted to hear, and from the look on her mother's face, she knew she'd said the right thing.

"I was so worried I hadn't expressed myself properly."

"No need to worry about that. Whatever you wanted to say came through exactly as you intended."

Her mother sighed with relief. Her eyes were wider without eyelashes and Marlene couldn't bear looking into them.

"When the time comes, I want you to read it. You will, won't you, Marlene?"

Marlene dipped her spoon in the egg drop soup. The strands attached, detached in the cloudy broth. "Of course." She pushed the bowl away and gulped some lukewarm tea. "I think we should talk about something else."

When the waiter returned, he removed the soup bowls and brought their combination plates. Her mother's shrimp had a thick gelatinous grayish coating; her orange chicken was shellacked with pineapple bits and glazed maraschino cherries.

Neither of them had an appetite. Marlene excused herself to go to the bathroom and threw up the little she'd managed to put away.

"It no good?" The waiter frowned at the barely touched plates of food.

"Everything was fine. We'll just take a check. My daughter will take both of these home."

On the way home, Marlene stopped the car and tossed the food in a garbage can.

CHAPTER FIFTEEN

Two months after her lunch with her mother, Marlene called Roseann to tell her that her mother had passed during the night.

"Pashed," Roseann repeated to the four women who'd gathered at her house to make plans for attending the funeral, "like she'd walked frough a gate." Roseann's speech had improved; it was still slushy but clearer.

"The heavenly gate," Susan murmured, "through which we will all pass if we're lucky. I'd rather pass through Saks and get trampled when they're having a sale."

"Marlene is too sensible to believe in that crap," Barbara said. "We should probably send flowers."

"She's Jewish," Grace noted. "I don't think we should send flowers. I think if we all chipped in and sent food that would be appropriate." Grace had Jewish clients in her bereavement group. "Or we could each make a meal."

Susan immediately nixed that idea. "I could call Bruno's deli and have them deliver a platter. Marlene said they would be having people back to the house after services, and I assume that means lunch."

The others agreed to that plan. Susan would call the deli. As for how to get to the funeral, that took a bit more negotiating. Barbara said she would drive to the funeral, but she would not be able to go to the cemetery. "I have to leave right after the services. Hank needs my car. His is in the shop." She avoided looking at Grace.

Grace had decided to tell Barbara she was considering moving to a place closer to the agency. She hoped Barbara would understand, but it wasn't the real reason. The real reason was she was uncomfortable being around Hank. She avoided him as much as possible, but it was difficult to pretend that nothing had happened.

Susan offered to watch William and be at Marlene's to receive the platters of food. "I'll need a key to her house. I'm happy to set up tables and chairs."

"Yesh. Good. Talk to Marlene about shetting shings up. She might have shome inshrushons about how she wans shings done. And Al too."

Susan nodded in Roseann's direction.

"The question now is what should we wear," Susan pondered aloud. With her, it was always a question of what would be most flattering as well as appropriate.

"Anything black, I suppose," Grace suggested. "I don't think there are any set rules for Jewish funerals."

Susan sighed. "That's all I wear lately anyway. I've gained ten pounds since I started dating Gary." All that pasta was playing havoc with her waistline.

"Well, you certainly don't look it," observed Barbara "You could use a few extra pounds."

"Some people eat when they are unhappy, others shut down," Grace said reaching for another chocolate chip cookie, then slapping her own hand away.

"I'm jush glad I'm alive. I plan to eat whatever I friggin' want," Roseann said cheerfully.

CHAPTER SIXTEEN

The funeral hall was one quarter filled with the few remaining elderly relatives and friends Marlene's mother had kept up with through the years. Marlene's daughter Bonnie sat with her three children, the children playing with their cell phones even though their mother had warned them she would confiscate them if they turned them on during the services. Bonnie's husband Jerry attended his mother-in-law's funeral for his wife's sake. Jerry was very handsome while Bonnie, to be honest, was rather plain, even dowdy looking. Marlene recalled her mother taking Bonnie aside to express her doubts about their forthcoming marriage.

"I don't think he'll be around for long," she'd told her granddaughter at the engagement party. "That kind is too good-looking for his own good and marries a plain woman to make himself look better. You be careful."

Marlene was infuriated when Bonnie repeated what her grandmother had said. The next day she called her mother. "Why did you say that to Bonnie? They are in love. They seem perfectly happy. That was a terrible thing to say to her. She is so upset, she called me in tears."

"That Bonnie is too sensitive," her mother answered. "I was just being honest."

"Well, you keep your honesty to yourself," Marlene fumed.

Bonnie never got over the insult. She didn't want her to come to the wedding. Marlene told her daughter to ignore her grandmother.

"She didn't like your father either when she met him. And see how wrong she was?"

Marlene's mother had been right about Bonnie's husband Jerry, who'd turned out to be a serial womanizer, and oddly enough, the women he fooled around with were plain as milk toast. Bonnie knew she was still number one in his life. She made her peace with his faults for the sake of the children who loved and needed their father.

In time Bonnie also forgave her grandmother. There was no sense holding a grudge when her grandmother had been right all along. Now she sat stoically next to her granddad, who sat in the first row next to his sister Constance, who'd had a falling-out with Marlene's mother years ago, the reason long forgotten. Marlene's Uncle Irving, her mother's brother, was too ill to make it to the funeral but said he would watch it on Zoom, except no one had thought to set it up.

Marlene glanced behind her. The mah jongg group sat together and waved when they saw her. She nodded in recognition and blinked away tears. Al sat next to her. He was wearing a dark double-breasted suit, a white shirt Marlene had ironed that morning, and a thin black tie that, he claimed, was the same one he'd worn at both his parents' funerals.

When it was time for Marlene to go to the bimah and read the eulogy, Al patted her hand and whispered, "You'll do fine. Just remember to look up and at the audience from time to time."

Unsteady, a tissue balled in her fist, Marlene got up and walked to the podium where someone adjusted the microphone.

She cleared her throat and began by describing the lunch at Chang's Garden. "The purpose of the lunch was to go over the eulogy she'd written that I will read to you."

There was some shuffling of feet as the congregants leaned forward to hear Marlene. Roseann grabbed Grace's hand. "Can you believe thish?" she stage-whispered.

"Be quiet," Barbara scolded.

Roseann blew her nose and dabbed her eyes with an old tissue she found in her handbag.

"Mama insisted we meet at her favorite restaurant to make sure her eulogy was clearly written. That's exactly what she told me when I balked at editing it." Marlene smiled. "Guess she was concerned there might be some grammatical mistakes and she wanted to put my college education to good use."

A polite chuckle ran through the audience.

Marlene unfolded the typed piece of paper and pretended to read what she could have easily recited by heart. Nervous, she stumbled over the first few words.

"I want to say . . . I want to say . . . that I am not afraid of dying. When it is time, we must all be prepared to take that last step, which is to be thankful for what life has given us." Marlene paused. "I am thankful for my lovely home, my little garden where I always found peace, and for the friends and family who have cared for me these past months. I know that I have received more than I ever hoped for in my life." Marlene teared up, her voice falling before continuing. "My needs were simple, and they have been fulfilled by those I love. Thank you all for coming."

Marlene was about to step away from the podium and return to her seat when something stopped her. She struggled to hear what she believed was her mother's voice channeling through her.

Marlene stared at the stolid, implacable coffin and knew there was more she was meant to say. But what? Her mother's lips were sealed like her coffin. The congregation grew restless.

Marlene cleared her throat. "There is more I forgot to read." She turned to the blank side of the eulogy she had just recited.

"I cannot leave this world without thanking my daughter Marlene for all her kindness and compassion in my darkest hours. Not once did she complain or disappoint me. Up until now I was unable to express what I wanted to tell her. Know, dearest Marlene, that you have my eternal love and gratitude." Marlene looked for her father. She hesitated an instant and continued. "And to you, David, my life's companion, I offer all my thanks for the wonderful years we had together. Thank you for your devotion, your loyalty, and your love. Bless you always."

The congregation murmured its approval. The rabbi rested his hand on her shoulder. "That was lovely." He walked her to the end of the bimah, and when she returned to her seat Al was grinning ear to ear. "I got to hand it to you."

Marlene reached past Al and pressed her father's shoulder. "Are you okay, Dad?"

He grimaced. "Did she really write that?"

"Yes. Of course she did. She loved you, Pop, with all her heart and soul. That's what she told me the day we went out for lunch." Did God care that she was crossing her fingers for a good cause?

CHAPTER SEVENTEEN

Susan and Gary were again meeting at Armando's. Gary really loved the pasta. Susan still wasn't sure about her feelings for Gary Rheingold. She'd convinced herself she wasn't looking for a serious relationship. They still hadn't had sex although there had been cuddling. She was disappointed but wasn't it better to enjoy the slow pace he'd set rather than plunge into and possibly drown in deep waters? They were adults, after all, although they didn't have all the time in the world.

She undressed, tossed her clothes on a leather chair in the corner of her small bedroom, and walked naked into the bathroom, where she took off her makeup, brushed her teeth, dabbed night cream around her eyes—*damn crow's feet*—and massaged moisturizer on her face and under her chin, working it down her neck and circling her breasts.

She tossed four throw pillows on top of her discarded clothes and drew the shades to shut out the view of the complex's parking lot. Like the rest of her condo, the bedroom was furnished simply with modern pieces she'd purchased over time: a white laminate dresser with cut glass—well, plastic resin, but they passed for glass—knobs, a computer desk and ergonomic leather chair, twin night tables, and a queen-size platform bed that, she realized too late, was too low and too hard for a comfortable night's sleep. But she'd adjusted. She'd kept the antique lamps and gilt mirror from her marriage to her second husband. They'd been purchased when honeymooning in Paris before he lost all their money in a Ponzi scheme. She sighed as she crept under the covers and reached for the clicker.

Recently, she'd splurged on a large high-end Samsung TV, an intruder she allowed to invade her privacy a few hours each night. She arranged her head on the pillows, hoping to block out thoughts that would interfere with sleeping. But she wasn't successful. Okay, you weren't supposed to use your devices before turning in, but she hadn't turned off her cell phone in case Gary called to say what a wonderful evening they'd had. But he hadn't called yet. She dialed his number, deciding she'd make the next move and invite him for dinner this coming Friday.

"I'd love to come," he said, "but could you make it Saturday instead?"

She wanted to ask him why not Friday but decided not to. "Of course," she said.

Now Saturday had come, and she was putting the final touches on the meal. In anticipation of their dinner, she'd gone out of her way to prepare his favorite dish, pasta primavera. She hadn't cooked in ages, but she found she enjoyed fussing in the kitchen, surfing the internet for recipes, and dusting off old recipe books she, for some reason, hadn't discarded. In the end, she'd called Roseann, who was a fabulous cook, to ask for a recipe.

"Well, this sounds serious," Roseann had said quite clearly. The speech therapy was doing wonders.

"Not really. I just thought—"

"Let me call you back."

"Or you can just text me."

Roseann laughed. "I'll ask William when he comes home from school. You coming to mah jongg Tuesday? Marlene's house."

"Yes, I'll be there. How are you doing, Roseann? Do you want me to pick you up?"

"Yes. Good luck with your dinner. If you want, I'll be your waitress."

Susan had laughed. "Thanks, hon. But two's company and three's—"

"A pain in the ass."

Susan was so glad Roseann was back to her old self.

Susan was nervous about how the meal would turn out. But everything looked good—and she hadn't burned the sauce that simmered fragrantly on the stove.

Gary brought flowers and a light Italian wine. He complimented her on her cooking skills. "Looks and smells amazing," he said, lifting the pot cover. "May I taste?"

"Of course."

"Mmmm. But it could use a little more salt."

She handed him the saltshaker. "Go right ahead. I'm afraid my taste buds are a bit out of practice." She explained that this was her first real homecooked meal in years. "My microwave and I are on the best of terms. I think my stove was in shock when I turned on the burners."

He added the salt, tasted the sauce again, and asked for the pepper shaker. "I appreciate the effort and you should consider doing this more often. For practice."

"Practice makes perfect," she teased, winking. *Really! Does he mean he wants me to cook for him more often? I like doing this for him tonight but definitely not on a regular basis.* "I would be happy to do it again, but only if you are my sous chef."

She lit the candles before they sat down. He uncorked and poured the wine. "This is terrific, Susan. How did you know pasta primavera is my favorite?"

"Because you've ordered it twice when we've eaten out, and I have this extraordinary memory. Some more pasta?"

He groaned. "I'm done. Excellent, though."

"Room for dessert? I bought cannoli from a local Italian bakery. The owner said they were absolutely authentic. They're filled with ricotta, nuts, and citron."

"I could never say no to an authentic or inauthentic cannoli. My grandmother used to make her own, and when I was a kid, I helped with the filling—that is, I licked the bowl."

"Well, these are bakery bought. How about an espresso? I have one of those overpriced machines I bought before I got divorced. I'm not sure I remember how to use it."

"I think I would prefer a refill on the wine." He and Susan reached for the bottle at the same time. He held her hand and she did not make a move to release it. By the time he finally let go, she'd made up her mind to sleep with him.

After dessert, he suggested they watch the news, but because the news was so depressing, she suggested they look for some silly romantic movie.

"Something Italian?" she suggested. "In keeping with the theme."

She did a quick search on Netflix, and it was just luck, or serendipity, that the opening scene was a couple groaning and gyrating. Susan moved in, resting her head on Gary's shoulder and circling his ear with her tongue.

"Is this what you want?" he asked.

"Don't you?" she whispered, reaching for him. Her voice was husky. "I think we both want it. We've waited long enough."

Her fingers strayed to his crotch. She was wet, tingling with desire. Gary was still soft. "There now," she coaxed, murmuring his name—Gary, Gary, Gary. "We could go into the bedroom or if you're more comfy here . . ."

"Whatever you want."

"No, sweetie, whatever you want. It's your call."

When he didn't make a move, she took his hand and led him into the bedroom, tugging ever so gently at his belt when they neared the platform bed. He offered no resistance when she began undressing him. When he was down to his jockeys, she lifted her blouse and undid her lacey bra. Her nipples were hard like the tips of pencil erasers.

With a bit of effort—her back was still killing her from Pilates—she eased herself very slowly onto the platform bed, all the while staring up at him. The room was dark, but not so dark he couldn't see her.

"Gary? Honey. I'm here." She held out her arms. He plopped down beside her. He took a minute to get the idea that she wanted him to ride her. Or at least get into the saddle.

Turning on her side, she thrust her left nipple in his mouth.

Suck, you bastard, she thought. She wanted to scream, "What's going on? Don't you want this?"

The men she had sex with appreciated, encouraged her aggressiveness. She discovered that what men wanted was the challenge, the excitement of fulfilling her needs while satisfying their own urges. It heightened the foreplay when she teased them, tantalized them with her demands. She was prepared to please Gary.

"It's okay," she assured him when she realized she had better take the lead. Poor guy was so shy. She massaged his body, tracing the gap between his thighs with her fingertips until she found his penis, no longer limp. *Thank God.*

"May I?" She very gently rubbed his balls, then kissed them, her saliva pooling on his pouch. "Mmmm." She licked him, waiting for some response. "Don't you like this?"

"Yes," he finally gasped.

"Then show me."

Susan wrapped her legs around him and gyrated like a whirlybird. When he climaxed, she expected that, in time, he would go down on her. Then ride her. Together they would gallop around *her* corral.

She waited and waited, knowing men needed time to regenerate. But how long would he take? *Come on, sweetheart. My turn.* She was a pressure cooker about to explode. Finally, she grabbed him by the shoulders. "Go for it," she shouted. Then pleading, "Gary, please, baby."

"Gary?"

He had turned away, put his head on his pillow, closed his eyes. "So tired," he slurred, yawning.

Done. Finis.

Susan cursed. Why had she seduced him? she asked herself. The truth was, she wanted to sleep with him more out of curiosity than desire. She should have waited for Gary to initiate sex, but she hadn't because there was something gnawing at her. She wanted to know what it felt like to be with a man who believed only the perfect woman was good enough for him. She wanted to show him she was that kind of woman. On one level she was successful. She'd aroused him, but there was no passion. Somehow, she'd failed him. Once he climaxed, the game was over. He didn't want her. He'd turned away and shut her out.

Susan went into the bathroom. Slamming the drawers, she found her vibrator but failed to reach an orgasm. It was all her fault, she told herself. She was too aggressive, too needy. This wasn't the behavior of the perfect woman. She'd behaved like a slut, and she wouldn't be surprised if he never called her again.

Susan crept back into bed and watched the rise and fall of Gary's narrow chest. What was he dreaming about? She doubted the dreams had anything to do with her. Awhile later when he awoke, he found her staring at him. "Are you okay?"

"Yes. Absolutely," she lied. "You fell asleep. I didn't want to disturb you."

"Hard day. Dinner was great, particularly the dessert."

Did he mean the sex?

He left around midnight, offering to do the dishes and help her tidy up before going home.

"No, that's not necessary," she said, forcing a smile. "Go home. It's late."

"I'll call you tomorrow. Like I said, dinner was delicious."

"Glad you enjoyed it."

She got his coat. She'd text him later. Take a cue from that Marla Maples. What was it the woman said when she was asked by some journalist what it was like to have sex with the Donald? Splashed her answer in the headlines.

"Best I ever had," she'd said. *Yeah, but where is Marla Maples today?*

Gary kissed her on the cheek. "Next Saturday we can go out for dinner, maybe take in a movie."

"I'd like that." Then she remembered she had promised to babysit this coming weekend. "Oh, I entirely forgot I can't do Saturday or Sunday. I'm babysitting my grandkids. My daughter was invited to a weekend wedding in Vermont and will be staying over. But I could see you Friday."

"Sorry, I can't do Friday."

She frowned. "Sure. No Fridays, I forgot."

Susan spent the rest of the night pondering what had happened: his correcting the sauce, encouraging her to cook more often for him, her taking the lead and practically forcing him to have sex, his expecting to see her again but not on Friday. Never on Friday! Wasn't there a song like that? No, it was never on Tuesday. And he never offered a reason why Friday didn't work for seeing her.

Why was she so offended by the put-off? They both had busy lives and she was probably expecting too much. Like wanting the sex to be great. It would be better the next time, she told herself. They just needed to get to know each other better. It would take time . . . more Saturdays and Sundays. She giggled, having finished the wine and devoured what was left of the cannoli.

Why the hell should I feel guilty about my needs? I'm not promiscuous; I just wanted this man to want me as much as I wanted him. Isn't that expected of the perfect woman, Gary? A woman who desires and craves you as much as you desire and crave her?

Before closing her eyes, Susan punched the pillow where Gary had laid his head and drifted off to sleep. She realized she was crying and hated herself for feeling so let down. Who was he to her anyway?

CHAPTER EIGHTEEN

Two weeks after the funeral her father asked Marlene to meet him for breakfast at the Baycrest Diner, which was twenty minutes from her parents' house. She hadn't seen her father since the funeral although they'd talked on the phone. Marlene assumed he wanted to discuss selling the house. She wished he wouldn't; she couldn't face losing any more of her childhood. Her mother's death was too fresh. But it was, after all, his decision, so she would try to be helpful.

Funny, but she was unable to recall a single time she and her father had ever been in a restaurant without her mother being present. It felt awkward, like meeting someone from your past and getting reacquainted. She supposed they would have to learn how to talk to one another without the mediation of her mother. And that might be a positive.

Seated opposite him in the booth, Marlene realized her father looked the same way he always looked. There was no stress or grief etched on his face. He was clean-shaven after the seven days of sitting shiva, dressed casually in a pair of khakis and a mustard-colored plaid shirt. The shirt looked like it had been retrieved from the hamper—the tips of the collar were curled, grazing the sagging folds of his neck. It was foolish to think he'd still be wearing the mourner's black ribbon that had been pinned to the lapel of his black suit. According to custom, she had burned her ribbon and given the black skirt and black blouse she'd worn for seven days to Goodwill. Should she suggest going back to the house to pack up her mother's things and donate them as well? Maybe it was too soon to bring up getting rid of her mother's things.

When she'd arrived, her father had already picked out a booth. He asked, "How was the drive down?"

"I hit some traffic when I got to the Cross Westchester. They're working on fixing the potholes so there was a tie-up, but it wasn't too bad."

There was a long pause while his face disappeared behind the menu, giving her time to think about how to bring up the subject of the house if he didn't bring it up first.

When the waitress came over, her father ordered a western omelet, no onions, and a sesame bagel, then balked at having to pay extra for the bagel as a substitution for toast.

Marlene shook her head; some things never change. "My father will have the bagel, and I'd like two eggs over easy and unbuttered wheat toast."

She waited, feigning interest in the diner décor, waiting for her father to say something, anything, about his plans.

"How are Al and Bonnie?"

"Bonnie is fine. You should give her a call. I know she'd love to hear from you," Marlene lied. Bonnie and her grandfather had never been close. She hated the way he disrespected her grandmother whenever her grandparents came to visit or she stayed over their house.

"Al still volunteering with the fire department?"

"Yes."

"Man never should have retired."

"Al enjoys his retirement. He keeps very busy. And he was just promoted at the fire station."

"As a volunteer. Hogwash. Still had a few good years ahead of him. Should have done something on the internet. Al missed the boat retiring at his age, if you ask me."

Well, she wasn't asking, damn him. And she wasn't about to defend her husband, whom her father didn't think much of. Al wasn't a go-getter. As far as he was concerned, Marlene's decision to marry Al was another example of her defiance, her willfulness. She'd written a blueprint for disappointment.

Her mother had agreed with her husband. "You should have married a doctor or a lawyer," she had told her, never failing to report the successful men her friends' daughters had latched on to. Their daughters lived in fancy houses and took expensive vacations. Their grandchildren went to private schools and were guaranteed places in Ivy League schools, whereas her daughter had settled for Al, who didn't have the same ambition as those other sons-in-law.

Her parents had thrown up their hands in disgust when she said she'd made up her mind. Al was the one. Why? He was honest, sweet, kind, respectful, fun to be with, and he loved her. That's why.

Marlene knew she'd made the best choice, never regretted marrying Al. She just hoped her mother had realized what a good person Al was before she died.

When the waitress returned with their orders, her father broke off a piece of bagel and dipped it into his egg.

"Aren't you eating?" he asked.

"Guess I'm not hungry."

Marlene's stomach was in knots. She pushed the food around her plate. *Why do I have the distinct feeling he is holding back, that he wants to tell me something?*

"Dad," she plunged ahead, "is there something on your mind? A reason you wanted to see me?"

Her father rested his fork on the edge of his plate, reached into his jacket pocket, and handed her an envelope. The letter was addressed to him, postmarked a week ago. She turned to the flap and read the return address. *Mrs. Betty Gross, St. Petersburg, Florida.* Marlene did not recognize the name. A letter of sympathy from one of her parents' friends? She withdrew two sheets of paper. The first was from World Travel confirming two bookings on a seven-day cruise to Nassau set to depart in three weeks from Miami.

She was surprised, but taking a vacation after the stress of losing your wife was not a bad idea, if a bit premature. And her mother had been ill such a long time. She couldn't blame her father if he needed some relaxation after what he'd had to deal with.

Marlene scanned the accompanying letter. She read it twice. A knot formed in her stomach. She was so taken aback by the content she could barely get the words out. "How long have you known this woman?" she sputtered.

"Long enough."

"Did Mom know about this?"

"She knew. Marlene, I want you to understand something. Your mother and I, it's been years since we loved one another. I was planning to leave her but then she got sick . . . I needed to get on with my life."

Marlene cut him off. She put her palms over her ears.

"Marlene, I'm trying to tell you something."

"Don't. I don't want to hear this." She glared at her father. If looks could kill he'd be dead. Her teeth clenched. "Well, you certainly didn't waste any time, did you, *getting on with your life*? It's a shame you wasted your money because according to this Betty, she's stated very clearly that she can't accept your invitation. In fact, from the sound of it, she's calling the whole affair off. She's asked you not to call her. I think she's made her intentions quite clear."

Her father shrugged his shoulders. "Oh, Betty's said that before. She'll change her mind."

Marlene's voice rose a few octaves. "I don't believe this. I honestly don't believe this. What the fuck were you thinking, Dad? You arranged this little vacation while Mom was dying! You shit, you."

The couple at the next table turned their heads and began whispering.

"Marlene, you better watch your language."

"Don't *you* tell me what to do." Tears stung her eyes. "All the time Mom was sick, dying, you and this woman. She knew. Mom knew and never let on. Oh, God." She broke down. Eggs, toast, coffee—it all was choking her. "I'm going to throw up," she heaved.

Her father's tone became gentler, more conciliatory, realizing the blow he'd struck. "Marlene, sweetheart, let me explain."

"Explain? Don't bother." Marlene pushed her plate away so forcefully her fork clattered to the floor. Bending down to get it, she could feel the blood rush to her face, and, for a second, she was so dizzy she was afraid she'd faint. When she retrieved the fork, she set it back on the table and just stared at it. *I would stab him with this fork. I would stab him right through the heart if it would make things any better. I would do it for you, Mom.*

The waitress reappeared and offered to top off their mugs with hot coffee. Marlene brushed her aside. The interruption gave her time to regain control. She took a cleansing breath. "Why, why are you showing me this?"

"Because I need your help. I want you to write a reply."

Had she heard right? She couldn't believe what her father was asking. "You . . . you . . . want me to write a letter asking this woman to change her mind? To see you? To go away with you?"

Her father nodded. "I know how Betty thinks. She's just feeling guilty."

"Why in heaven's name would you ask me to do this?"

"Because I know you wrote your mother's eulogy, and you would know what to say."

Marlene flushed. She felt trapped in her deceit. "I did not write Mom's eulogy," she protested. "Mom wrote her eulogy. She asked me to see if it was clear, that's all."

"You're lying. I know your mother, Marlene. She didn't write all of it. I saw the eulogy when she first wrote it. She showed it to me. She wanted my opinion. I know you added that last part. Didn't you? The part about me being such a wonderful husband."

Marlene buried her face in her hands. "Yes," she whimpered.

"So now, my dear daughter, you can do this for me. Tell Betty how much I need her. Tell her that together we can start a new life. I know she will change her mind because you'll find the right words to convince her."

"No. I can't. You can't make me. Why would I do this?"

He rested his hand on hers. His eyes were pleading. She had never known her father to look at her like this. "Yes, you will. You'll do it because my whole life I've been dying and now I want to live."

CHAPTER NINETEEN

Although she wasn't playing mah jongg because it was too difficult for Roseann to focus on the patterns and, too often, she'd mistake a Bam for a Crak when she discarded a tile, she insisted on hosting Tuesday's game. William was off from school, and he set up the card table and chairs in the family room. He hung around watching the women (he now considered aunts) play this incomprehensible game until a friend called and invited him to his house. Video games made a lot more sense, he decided.

The women insisted on bringing snacks—cheese and crackers, almonds, veggie sticks and hummus—and, as it had become a new tradition, Susan brought a bottle of wine for anyone who wanted to imbibe. Usually it was Susan, Grace, and Barbara, although that day Marlene agreed to "just a drop."

The women sipped their wine while Marlene related her breakfast with her father. She did not miss a detail because it was good to get everything off her chest. She had been too mortified to tell Al what had occurred. Since he and her father had never liked each other, this would only make their relationship even more acrimonious—something she wanted to avoid now that her mother was gone.

"He did what?" Susan's back stiffened with the shock of what Marlene was telling them. "He booked tickets for a cruise with this Bethy woman while your mother was dying?"

"Betty. And yes, he showed me the confirmation with the dates, and then he showed me the letter she had written saying she was not going on the cruise to Nassau. That, in fact, she no longer wanted to see him. She was too filled with guilt."

"Good for her." Barbara raised a fist. "I like this woman."

"And he asked you to write a letter where he apologized for making her feel bad. To say he understood her feelings blah, blah. To do this since you had written your mother's eulogy." Grace was trying to get all the details right. Clearly Marlene was devastated. This was a problem that went deeper than Marlene understood.

Susan was irate. "The fuckin' nerve. Leave it to a man to screw not only his wife but his mistress, and then to expect both to forgive him. Tony, my first husband, was balling the nanny, and when she became pregnant, he wanted me to go with her when she had the abortion. To hold her hand, can you believe?"

"You didn't, did you?" Marlene asked, horrified at the idea.

"Actually, I said I would go only because Lauren was the best nanny we'd ever had, and I didn't want to lose her. I didn't agree with her having the abortion, and when she changed her mind, I said I would keep both her and the baby. Joy loved having the baby around. She didn't know for years the baby was her half-brother. Things get so complicated." Susan sighed, still thinking about her frustrating tryst with Gary.

"I would think so."

"Marlene, will you let Susan finish," Barbara demanded, sick of all the interruptions. Why is it they could never stick to one topic? They'd been talking about Marlene's breakfast and now it was all about what happened to Susan's nanny God knows how many years ago.

"Lauren and I still keep in contact. She tells me John is applying to college—I can't believe it—naturally, she can't get a dime out of Tony to pay his tuition, which doesn't surprise me in the least." Susan took another sip of wine. "I paid for Joy's on my own, and it was a struggle."

"We women do what we need to do," Grace said. She was still paying off loans for her twins' college tuition. With her salary as a clinical social worker it would take eons to make a dent. But she had hopes of adding more clients to her private practice.

"Well, I wouldn't have been as forgiving." Roseann was thinking about Cindy's behavior, about her abandoning her son and husband, running off to Boulder with some guy from work. She still hasn't heard from Eric, who dropped out of the rehab program. He could be anywhere; he could be (she shuddered) dead.

Forgiveness. Barbara was not happy about Grace renting an apartment on the other side of town. Grace had also intimated that she was too busy to play in her regular game. Too polite, too ethical to give the real reason she was distancing herself from Barbara. Grace said her private practice was growing and she had to be available for more clients. It meant Barbara had to look for a new tenant. She doubted she'd find one as responsible as Grace.

"So, what are you planning on doing, Marl? Are you going to write that letter?"

"I haven't decided, Susan."

The room got very quiet. Marlene looked at each of the players. "What do you all think I should do?"

"Well, I would write the letter," Barbara said. "He is, after all, your father."

"Grace?"

"It depends on how you feel about writing the letter."

"What a shrink thing to say. *How does this make you feel?*" Susan mimicked. She had been to enough shrinks to know the script.

Grace ignored the jab. "So how *do you feel* about helping your father?"

"I feel it sucks!" Marlene responded.

"Do you feel like you would be dishonoring your mother's memory?" Grace questioned.

Marlene shrugged. "No, maybe. I don't know."

Barbara got up and went to refill her wine glass. She really had to watch herself or she'd wind up like Hank, trying to escape the present with pills and booze. "Honestly, can we just play mah jongg and stop this psychotherapy crap?"

Roseann raised a hand. "I think it's a good thing that we discuss Marl's problem. Isn't that what we're here for? To help one another?"

"Absolutely," the others agreed.

"What would you do, Rosie?" Marlene titled her head in Roseann's direction.

"I told you. I wouldn't write the letter."

"Susan?"

"I wouldn't either."

"Barbara?"

"Like I said, he's your father and from what you said, your mom already knew what was going on. Besides which, she's dead and he deserves a second chance at living. He told you that himself. So what's the harm?"

"Grace?"

"I'm neutral."

Susan guffawed. "Oh yeah, here we go again with the perfect shrink answer."

"So, what is it going to be?" Barbara frowned.

"I don't know. I really don't know."

"Let's not pressure her, okay? Knowing Marlene, she'll wind up doing the right thing in the end." Grace smiled her most engaging smile at Marlene, who said, "You know what?"

"What?" everyone except Barbara chimed together.

"I need a group hug. You guys are the best . . . Come here, Barb. You're part of this group."

CHAPTER TWENTY

"It's a shame you are leaving the cottage after the way you fixed it up," Marlene said. She was the fifth and waiting her turn to play the next game. "The place feels so comfy without being overdone." She gulped, wishing she could eat her words. Was that a deliberate jab at Susan whose apartment was so . . . what did she call it? . . . holistically balanced or some such nonsense?

Grace had decorated with lots of color, giving one the feeling the room was aglow with sunshine, even on a gloomy day like today when the rain trickled from the eaves, plop-plopping on the rust-freckled drainpipes. The upholstery on the sofa and companion loveseat was striated red and orange. There were throw pillows in rainbow colors and a jumbo tufted yellow floor-pillow lounger for watching TV or just taking a nap. Grace had a passion for handcrafts. She went to local fairs and craft shows and had an impressive collection of hand-blown vases and terracotta ceramics filled with dried flowers and reeds.

"I love all these planters," Marlene said, examining a turquoise pot hosting flowering geraniums Grace had rescued from a neighbor's garbage bin. "Your new place have this much sun?"

"I'm not sure. I hope the plants will survive the move." Grace looked up from the mah jongg tiles she'd been passed from Barbara, considering a five Bam that would work for a consecutive run. She sighed. This was probably going to be the last mah jongg game she'd be playing with these women who she'd grown so close to. She also wished she wasn't going to leave the cottage. There were the twins' outstanding college loans, and the new apartment was going to cost her an extra fifty dollars a month. The extra days she'd be working at the VA would help, but there would be nothing left over to indulge in hobbies like taking a pottery course and throwing pots. Unless she could sell what she made. There she went again, blue-skying.

Marlene picked up a cracker and cheese. "It must be difficult to start over. I can't imagine Al and me moving from our house. Thinking about packing all the stuff we have is daunting. Al, unfortunately, is a packrat. I shiver thinking about what he's collected over the years and kept in cartons in the basement."

Susan stared at the three tiles she'd just received from Roseann. Did Roseann really mean to pass her two Flowers? She was worried about Roseann. Ever since her stroke she was losing her concentration and possibly having difficulty seeing. Not that she or the other women would say anything. What had happened to Roseann could happen to anyone.

Marlene was still babbling. "I just love it here. You've made it so . . . welcoming. And I'm sure Barbara is going to miss having you as her tenant."

Susan arched an eyebrow, wishing the damn woman would just shut up and let them play.

"Thank you," Grace said simply, passing three tiles in the crossover to Barbara, who exclaimed, "I haven't gotten one decent tile in this entire Charleston. Someone give me something decent."

"I will miss living here. But my new place is much closer to the VA hospital and the social service agency, and I will probably have to stay late to see clients who work during the day." The director of the agency had offered her the position of manager of their vocational program. It meant coming in earlier to set up internships for the clients and being on call if they had problems at their jobs.

"How is your practice going?" Marlene asked.

"I'm busier than ever and loving it." Last week she had a new referral for marriage counseling. This couple looked more promising than the first one she'd counseled: the husband had stormed out of the office, claiming Grace was siding with the *bitch*. She wasn't sure how she could fit everything in, but she needed to build her private practice even if it meant more evening and weekend work in order to pay off the twin's college loans.

"It's the optional. Roseann, what do you have?" Susan tapped her finger lightly on the card table.

Roseann jerked her head and stared blankly at her rack. "Oh, maybe one. No, two. I'm not sure."

"Can you just pass me something? Anything? Please. I have shit."

Susan reached into her blazer pocket, feeling a slight vibration from her cell. He had called once after dinner at her house, and she half-expected Gary to call again to arrange another get together. But he hadn't, and the time he did call he had just talked about his trip to Chicago and how nice it was catching up with friends and family. He hadn't asked her out, so she assumed the relationship was kaput. *Just as well.*

Barbara's voice sounded tight. "Grace, are you ready to discard? Your house, remember. You're East."

"Sorry." Grace discarded a three Dot. Barbara looked at it. Was it too early to call? She needed a three Dot but that meant using her Joker, which she really should save. She let the three Dot go.

The game turned out to be a Wall game. Marlene was ready to replace Roseann when there was a knock, no, a pounding at the door.

"Who could that be?" Barbara wondered aloud. Hank was staying with his brother Barry in Rhode Island. The two men had always gotten along, and since their separation, he'd been living and working with Barry, who had a construction company. It was just the kind of work Hank needed. And the separation was going to give her the break she needed. It meant more time to think about her future. She wasn't sure about staying in real estate. Meanwhile, she'd have to find a new tenant for the cottage. She and Grace had their issues, but Barbara had to admit, she'd never find anyone else who took such care or who was so responsible. *Damn Hank.* It was one more thing she held against him.

Grace got up. When she opened the door, Al rushed in like a bolt of lightning. "Where's Roseann?"

CHAPTER TWENTY-ONE

Al's face was red. He was huffing and puffing trying to catch his breath. "Where's Roseann," he sputtered. "I've got to speak to Roseann."

When Marlene heard his voice, she called out. "Al, we're in the living room, playing mah jongg." As soon as she saw him, she pushed her chair away and ran to her husband. She stood in front of him and grabbed his arm. "Are you okay? What's wrong? You're perspiring. Your face is flushed." She was constantly on the alert for a heart attack, even though the doctor assured her Al was doing fine. His pressure was under control and so was his cholesterol, thanks to Marlene's diligence—what Al called nagging.

Al extracted himself from his wife's clutches and put his hands on Roseann's shoulders. "Roseann, you better prepare yourself for a shock."

The rest of the women turned to Roseann. Her face had paled. "What . . . what ish it?"

"I had visitors. Eric and Cindy came to my house. They were looking for you. They thought you might be there since you and Marlene are such good friends."

"What, what do they want?" Her hands were shaking. She clutched the sides of the game table to steady herself from collapsing.

"They were asking about William and where he is. I told them you were at the doctor's and that William was on a camping trip."

"A camping trip?" Marlene's eyes widened. "A camping trip? In the middle of the winter? Al, what were you thinking?"

"That's the best I could come up with, Marl. I was on the spot. I don't think they believed me anyway. They're planning to go back to your house, Roseann."

"Eric has a key," Roseann said softly. Her breathing was labored.

"I don't think I can put them off, but I was thinking I would pick William up from soccer practice and take him somewhere," Al said.

"You're thinking about kidnapping William?" Marlene couldn't believe her ears. "Al, are you crazy?"

"Where are you thinking of taking him?" Susan asked.

"I don't know. Just away."

"Dr. Malcolm has a hunting lodge. I could call him and ask him if you could use it. I wouldn't have to explain why."

Barbara stared daggers at Susan. "This is not some TV crime series. You can't take William to some hunting lodge and hide him from his parents."

Grace stood up. She faced Al. She said firmly, "Al, Barbara is right. You can't hide William. Eric and Cindy are his parents and no matter what you think about them—"

"They're shits," Susan snarled. "Absolute shits. They can't do this to Roseann and William." She turned to Roseann, who had tears in her eyes. "William is so happy living with you. I don't trust those two. Don't let them take him, Roseann. Call the police. Get a restraining order."

Roseann put her hands up to stop Susan's harangue. "Please, everyone," she pleaded, "let Grace talk."

Grace waited a minute. She knew the shock could be too much for Roseann to handle and worried about her health. But she had to be clear for her sake and the sake of the child. "If you have concerns about Cindy and Eric as custodial parents, you can talk to social services and ask them to evaluate the situation. But you just can't arbitrarily deny his parents their rights to have their child unless there is evidence of abuse. There has to be cause . . . proof they are unfit, and then let the courts decide. I know this can take time and it will be frustrating. The bureaucracy is slow, but the courts are trying to do their best in the interests of the child. Do we know what William wants?"

"William will want to be with Cindy. He has been missing his mother, even though he stopped talking about her." Roseann bowed her head, unable to hold it up. Her whole body felt as if it was caving in. She didn't have the strength to get up from her chair; by rights she should be running to rescue her grandson.

Tears streamed down her face. "What am I going to do without that sweet little boy?"

Grace enfolded the distraught grandmother in her arms. Roseann was shaking, sobbing. "This is hard, very, very hard. But you have no choice." She spoke to Al over Roseann's head. "You better pick the boy up and bring him back. You shouldn't say anything about seeing his parents. Act natural. Roseann, I'll drive you home and we'll wait for Eric and Cindy. You are in no condition to do this by yourself. While we wait, we'll discuss what to say to William. We have to prepare William for seeing Eric and Cindy. We don't know how he will take this."

Roseann stepped away from Grace. She put her hands over her eyes and pressed her fingers into the sockets, shutting out reality, the future for the boy and for herself. She knew this would happen. It was only a matter of time before Eric came for William. But she did not expect to see Cindy again. She could fight Eric if she had to in the courts by pointing to his problems with addiction and the fact that he never completed his rehab. Cindy was different. She could make a case for having to leave William for her job. She was the mother doing the best she could to provide for her child. Who would criticize her for her actions? She'd gone to Boulder to make a fresh start for herself and her son. And now, she'd returned, possibly to reunite with her husband, the boy's father, in a final attempt to do what was best for William.

Roseann knew she had no recourse. She was only the grandmother, and she had no rights to take him away from Eric and Cindy, who might make a go of it. She had to think positively. She just prayed that the two would be good enough parents, good enough for her grandson, whom she loved more than life. What, what was she to do if they went back to their old ways? She didn't have an answer, only the broken heart of a sick woman who needed her grandson to be by her side.

CHAPTER TWENTY-TWO

Not knowing what Gary did on Fridays was like an itch Susan couldn't reach to scratch. She hated being so suspicious, but Gary was so mysterious.]Susan still hadn't a clue about what he did on Friday nights and why he never discussed it with her.

Tonight, at dinner—Gary cooked—she shared her concern about having to sell her condo and move in with her daughter and son-in-law. "It's not that I don't appreciate the effort they've made turning the garage loft into a mother-in-law apartment. I won't have to pay rent . . ." She frowned, lines etching around her mouth that needed a new shot of Botox. "But there is the downside of being a beck-and-call babysitter. Not that I don't absolutely adore my new granddaughter. I'm not good when they're newborns or toddlers. I'll like it when I can do things with my granddaughter, when she's older and I can take her shopping and we can go to a spa and have our nails done."

"What if she doesn't like doing that? What if she wants to go to a soccer or baseball game instead of going to a spa or whatever?" Gary asked.

"Don't be ridiculous," Susan pouted. "That won't happen if she has my DNA."

She took another sip of wine, hoping Gary wasn't mistaking her lack of interest in the football game for her lack of interest in him. She'd already finished more than her quota of the red wine he'd bought and was feeling the effects behind her eyes.

While he shouted at the TV, Susan leafed through a travel brochure that was lying on the coffee table. If only she had the money to get away somewhere, with or without Gary. There were so many trips on her bucket list. She would love to go on a safari to Africa, or sail on a junk in Southeast Asia. And there were all those Scandinavian countries to explore. She turned the pages, folding down the corners of the cruises that looked most inviting and out of reach. Maybe one day she could convince Gary to plan a trip. But right now, the furthest thing from Gary's mind was another trip abroad after ruining his knee, plus the expense. Another one of his complaints was how expensive things were when you traveled to foreign countries. Not that he couldn't afford it, Susan believed. He was turning out to be just a bit of a tight wad.

Gary was glued to the football game. Suddenly, he raised a fist and gnashed his teeth. "Damn it, man. What the fuck is wrong with you?" He jumped off the couch and practically tipped over the bottle of wine she caught, just in time, by its neck.

"What happened?" she cried, looking up from what looked like a perfect cruise to the Mediterranean, thinking maybe she could get Gary to return to his roots even though he'd already been there for the wedding. She'd always longed to visit Italy. Maybe he'd introduce her to his family. But she was getting way ahead of herself.

Gary was cursing under his breath. This was so unlike him. Gary, mild-mannered Gary, had never been so animated. If only he would show this much passion in bed.

"What's wrong?" she repeated.

"The guy fumbled the ball, and he will have just about lost the game is all."

"Oh. Sorry about that." *That's the way the cookie crumbles.*

She was not a big fan of football. In fact, she hated the way grown men piled on top of one another, intent on smothering each other to death or breaking each other's bones. And what about all those head injuries? She hated to think about the damage a stupid game caused because men had to prove how macho they were. Her granddaughter would never be into that!

"Game's over?" Susan asked when he shut off the TV.

"I'm getting another beer. Want anything?"

"No, thanks, honey. I'm okay with the wine. It was delicious, although I think I may have had a teeny bit too much. I feel a little tipsy and could use a bit of a lie-down." But her subtle invitation was lost on deaf ears. When Gary returned, he turned the TV back on and began surfing the channels for another game.

"Dr. Malcolm called," she began, waiting for a commercial break to tell Gary her news. "He wanted to know if I had any interest in coming back to work."

"Who is Dr. Malcolm?"

"I thought I told you. He's the dentist I used to work for. I was his receptionist. I quit because his wife was breathing down my neck. The jealous sow. Anyway, now the receptionist he hired to replace me is leaving." Susan was trying to see if her words were getting through to Gary, who continued to flip through the channels.

"Yeah, so?"

"So, apparently his wife is breathing down this one's neck now. Eliot, that's Dr. Malcolm, told me he was finally planning on divorcing her."

When Gary didn't respond—he seemed less interested in her news than she was in the football games—she continued, this time moving closer on the couch. "He's said that before, but this time I think he means it. So, what do you think? Should I take him up his offer and go back to work? That way I wouldn't have to move in with my kids. Gary . . ." She hesitated, not sure how this suggestion would go over. "Gary, honey, I was hoping I could move in with you. Just temporarily."

Now she did have his full attention.

"Gee, Susan," he faltered. "I don't know. This place is kinda small."

"Oh, I don't know. It's not that small. It could be quite cozy here if we rearranged some of the furniture. You have too much stuff. That Victorian settee for example . . . Why do you keep it? It's not even comfortable."

"It's a family heirloom. It was my grandmother's and her mother's before that."

"Say no more," Susan backtracked. "Still there must be some things you wouldn't mind parting with?"

Ever since she'd arrived, she'd been sizing up Gary's apartment. It was a small studio in a white brick prewar building that reminded her of her grandparents' apartment when she was growing up.

Susan used to visit her grandparents and sometimes stay over when her parents went on vacation. Even now, so many years later, she could recall the dark wood-paneled elevator and ornate iron-railing staircase going up the five steep flights and counting. She could picture herself counting the steps, never getting the same count, on her way to see Grammy and Grandpoppy. She recalled the exotic cooking aromas on each floor: the pungent curry of tagines, the fragrant oregano, basil, and garlic in simmering tomato gravy; the sweet smell of soy and ginger from her friend Hiro's apartment; and the heavenly yeasty smells of fresh bread called challah that made her mouth water every Friday.

Gary's apartment was on the fourth floor. She'd walked up all four in her new Prada four-inch spikey heels. Gary had insisted they forgo the elevator he didn't trust. "Besides which, it's good exercise," he claimed, climbing ahead of her.

Sure, if you want to break your ankles. What about that knee, she wondered, that never seemed to give him any trouble.

He'd furnished the studio with solid pieces of furniture he said he picked up at a hotel lobby furniture sale. The couch and easy chairs were upholstered in a faded tapestry fabric now worn on the arms. A rainbow afghan was thrown over the back to cover the greasy stains; she assumed his mother had crocheted it to keep her little Gary warm. Across from the couch was the horrible heirloom settee and between them a glass coffee table, scarred and chipped—he'd Scotch taped the raw edge, which Susan supposed was better than leaving it. Two orange ceramic lamps stood on matching wood laminate side tables recently bought online at IKEA. White metal blinds on the double window were set at half-mast. Dust-free, at least. The man liked his home pristine, which didn't surprise her. She doubted he had a cleaning person the way she did once a week. She'd die without her Maria.

The window looked out on a playground across the street where children's voices mingled with the noise of busy traffic. The building was on a main street with buildings of similar vintage on either side. Susan had an urge to untangle the cords to open the view and let in some natural sunlight, but Gary was very proprietorial, being a bachelor used to having things his way. That might be a problem if he agreed to let her stay with him.

The kitchen was small. Since Gary loved to cook, he had more appliances and pots and pans than Home Goods. The counter was cluttered with a wooden knife block, a toaster oven, coffee grinder, tower of coffee mugs, an electric tea kettle, a rice cooker, and a drain rack filled with dishes left to dry on their own. Gary did not have a dishwasher, which could be another problem. There were drawers of gadgets for slicing, dicing, and Lord knows what else.

"I'm impressed," she said when she'd earlier asked Gary to explain the use of what looked like a miniature guillotine.

"Bagel slicer. It saves cutting your finger accidently."

"Very clever." *What about the raw edges of the coffee table?* "And these?"

He'd explained the purpose of each gadget she held up, listening to his explanations.

"I had no idea a mango peeler and a strawberry huller were so useful. Absolutely ingenious. I bet these would save my manicure," she said, showing off the gel extensions of her nails.

Waiting for some response to her suggestion she move in with him, Susan tried to assure him it would be a temporary move. "I dread moving in with my kids. Not that I don't adore my family, don't get me wrong. Moving in with you, Gary, it would only be for a while. I'm seriously looking for an apartment that I can afford."

"I thought you loved being with your daughter. That you were very close."

"I do, but she has her family and I need my own space, Gary, and you know how it is when you move in with your adult children . . . but then you don't have any. Besides which, I really love being with you. I think we would really get along." She tilted her head, looking at him looking at her as if he were a deer in the headlights.

"It would only be for a short time," she kept repeating, hating the desperation she must be communicating. "Like I said, I'm thinking about going back to work now that Dr. Malcolm's wife won't be in the office. She's such a jealous person. So suspicious, always looking for something I'd done wrong instead of thanking me for basically holding the office together."

The truth was, Myrna Malcolm had cause to be jealous, questioning the credit card receipts when her husband was unable to account for the extended hotel stay and unexplainable restaurant charges in Bermuda when he said he was attending the American Dental Association conference. Myrna had been dogged in her pursuit of her husband's wrongdoing.

As for Susan's personal charges on the office credit card that were adding up like the stages of the Eiffel Tower, he'd had no excuses when Myrna presented him with the bill. Spa treatments, lunch and dinner at expensive restaurants they had never gone to. Take-out meals and charges to liquor stores.

Susan wondered what the dentist's reaction would be to the filmy black teddy tucked in her tote she had bought especially for tonight that had cost almost as much as what he charged for a root canal.

"Gary?" She waited for some response. Damn the man. Any other man would jump at the chance to have her live with him and have the privilege, value added, of on-demand sex.

"I'm not sure. Let me think about it, Susan."

Susan smiled her most winning smile. Nibbled her thumb nail and said coyly, "Great. What's for dinner? Nothing fattening, I hope. I'm starving."

"My famous vegetarian lasagna."

"I'll set the table. Where are the placemats? Now, you just sit back and relax and see if you can find another game to watch. I'll heat the lasagna."

"You sure you don't mind?"

"Of course not. Placemats?"

He pointed to the linen closet in the hallway. "Second shelf."

The closet was stuffed with sheets, towels, extra pillows, and blankets. How did one man accumulate so much stuff? But who was she to complain when she thought about all the cartons she'd had to put in storage. The shoes, sweaters, and coats she'd never wear but didn't have the heart to get rid of. It was probably costing her more in storage rental than the stuff was worth. When she moved in, she'd get rid of what Gary didn't need to make room for her things.

She found a stack of placemats on the top shelf and was removing two when she caught sight of a wooden box on the lower shelf that looked interesting. The box was obviously antique with tarnished brass hinges. She wondered what was in it. Of course, it was none of her beeswax. Yet . . .

She rested the box on the floor next to the two placemats and, on her knees, she began going through the contents, finding family photographs and memorabilia like old birthday cards, theater programs, and expired passports. After going through the first layer, she realized there was something underneath. These were not family photographs. Far from it. These were headshots of women printed off the computer.

"What the fuck?" Susan gasped. She felt her chest pounding the more she went through the cheaply printed photographs and read the accompanying profiles of women who had answered Gary's request for "Gal Fridays."

Some of the women were younger than she was, but many were photos of women who looked about her age. Clipped to the profiles were emails that had been exchanged. Susan checked the dates. Most of the emails were from the time before she and Gary had started dating, but, sorting them into matching sets (photos, profiles, emails) she realized that more than a dozen were dated more recently. One was only one week ago.

Her stomach turned. No, she was not going to vomit. She was going to gain control over herself. This was what occupied Gary on Fridays. The reason he had no time for her. Gal Fridays. Women Gary was seeking out in his quest for the perfect woman. Looking for more candidates. More choices. No, she was not going to scream. She was not that kind of woman. She was stronger than he was, and she was going to have the upper hand.

Susan put the box back exactly where she had found it. She'd confront Gary after dinner. After they made love.

Around nine o'clock, she yawned. "The game any good?" she asked, massaging his arm she had wrapped around her shoulder. She tilted her face up to his and fluttered her eyelashes.

"Not really."

"Want to do something a whole lot more interesting? I could think of a few things if you're up to it," she said. "Why don't you turn off the TV and come to bed. I have something to show you."

She picked up her tote bag and took out the scanty black teddy wrapped in tissue paper. "How about I model this?" she asked, unwrapping the teddy and holding it up. "I would love your opinion."

Gary followed her into his bedroom. Undressing slowly, pretending to be doing a striptease, she threw each article of clothing on the floor or in his face. Giggling, she stepped into the teddy and paraded around the room.

"Wow!"

"You like?"

The cutouts for her breasts were framed like portraits in shimmery ruffles, the slit in the panties outlined with faux fur. The outfit was far too expensive, but she'd been counting on it to arouse Gary, to take them to new heights.

When they lay down on his bed, she followed her routine of massaging his chest, his thighs, his balls, and fingering his cock. She did not offer to blow him. She was not that forgiving, the memory of her discovery extinguishing her sexual urges. Her pussy was dry as the Sahara Desert.

She didn't have to wait too long for Gary to climax as soon as he entered her and felt the tickle of the slit in the teddy. He stroked her hair and, as usual, being polite, he lifted himself above her and whispered his gratitude in her ear. "Thank you."

"You're welcome," she replied, hoping he didn't catch the sarcasm in her tone.

His snoring was deep and sonorous. His elbows were spread eaglelike, his fingers intertwined under his head. He slept without a care in the world while she tossed and smothered her anger in the pillow. How could he do this? How could he be so deceitful?

She did not blame Gary for being a disappointing lover. Not all close relationships were built on what went on in the bedroom. Sex was ephemeral and love eternal. Tony, her ex, was hot as hell, but a terrible husband and father. What she could not forgive was Gary's compulsion to find the perfect woman and to reject her as a candidate. She must have known from the beginning she was not really in the running. Yet, she thought she knew men. There had been so many in her life. And she had tried, believing the way to his heart was a ridiculous teddy and rich cannoli.

It was nearly midnight. Time to go home. Susan turned on her side and stared at the moonlight filtering through the slatted blinds that streaked like blurry rain on the wall. She cried softly while getting dressed in the dark and folded the teddy carefully in the original tissue paper. It seemed like such a waste to throw the ensemble in the garbage, even though it was gummy with his cum. She put it back in her tote. Waste not, want not.

Goodbye, Gary Rheingold. I hope you find her.

She closed the door to his apartment, took the elevator to the street floor, and found her car. Using her key to her condo, let herself in, took a shower, changed into her pajamas, and opened the small refrigerator.

There was the bottle of wine she was planning to take to Tuesday's mah jongg game. But she'd had enough wine already. *Damn. She hated Gary Rheingold. Would hate him forever.*

She was much too anxious to go to sleep; she logged onto her computer and searched for the dating website a girl in her yoga class had raved about. "It's very discreet. There are all kinds of screens before you actually get to go out with the person. I highly recommend it. The guys who pinged me were fab. Susan, you have got to try it."

Surfing the site, she decided on a trial membership and posted a photo Dr. Malcolm had taken of her when they were sailing in Bermuda. She looked trim and happy, with her hair blowing in the wind as she'd flirted with the camera and air-kissed her fingertips at him. He'd been blowing kisses back at her while focusing the iPhone camera, which accounted for the slight blurring of her features. Better than a close-up that revealed the age lines.

It took three attempts, but she finally settled on an updated profile that stated her interest in football and cooking. There. Take that, you bastard, she muttered pressing submit. She headed her posting *Gal Friday Looking for Companionship.*

CHAPTER TWENTY-THREE

"You must be so happy living here. Grace fixed the cottage up so beautifully. You're lucky to have inherited some of her furniture, Jennifer, and the plants she couldn't take with her," Susan said.

Jennifer was the new fifth and waited her turn to play the next game. Barbara had suggested her new tenant learn mah jongg and join the group.

"Do you like gardening?" Marlene asked.

Jennifer looked up from the mah jongg tiles she'd been studying like she was trying to translate Greek into English. If she passed Barbara a five Bam she might be giving up a possible consecutive run. But she wasn't sure. This game was so confusing. Why had she agreed to play mah jongg with these women with whom she had no connection?

"I'm afraid not," Jennifer said wearily. "I hope I don't kill these. I need to remind myself to water them. As for gardening, I have no time to do anything but work and go to school." Jennifer was an exercise physiologist. She was also studying to be a nutritionist and taking night classes at the community college. She sighed. "I love being with you all, but I'm afraid I'm not very good at this."

Susan was a member of Fitness Fulfillment and was so taken with Jennifer, who was the Pilates coach, she'd hired her for private lessons. When Jennifer told her she was looking for a place to live, she'd given her Barbara's contact information. Barbara was looking for a tenant and was immediately taken by the young energetic woman who offered, in exchange for a 5 percent reduction in rent, to have her join her exercise classes—either spinning or yoga—as often as she liked. Barbara went to Jen's workout classes whenever she could fit them into her schedule. The exercise was good for reducing stress as well as toning her body. Without Hank around, she had more time on her hands.

Marlene picked up a cracker and cheese and waited for Jennifer to throw a tile. Even Marlene was losing patience. Jennifer wasn't as sharp as Grace, and she didn't seem very enthusiastic about playing mah jongg. As for Roseann's coaching of Jennifer, there was a lot to be said for the advice she was getting. She looked at the three tiles again. Did Jennifer really mean to pass her a Joker?

"I just love it here. Grace made it so . . . welcoming and you, of course, have added your own touches." Susan turned to look at the wall that featured paint-sprayed shoes and a hat collection. "Creative, quite striking. Modern, abstract, like something you might see in a museum." *And not understand why it was there*, Susan silently added.

"Thank you," Jennifer said, passing three tiles in the crossover.

"It's to the right, Jen," Susan reminded the fitness guru who was much better at remembering exercise routines than remembering the Charleston. "We're not up to the crossover yet. Roseann, I thought you were helping her."

"I can't watch her every move, Susan."

Jennifer covered her eyes with her hand. She felt a migraine coming on. "Maybe I'm not cut out for mah jongg. I'm really, really sorry."

"Don't be silly," Susan said, trying to be sympathetic to the newcomer. "It just takes practice. You'll be fine." *In a hundred years.*

Marlene wished Grace were back playing in the game. She really missed her soothing presence. Whatever caused her to leave so abruptly? She'd offered plausible excuses, but there was something fishy about her leaving the game when she could have made time if she really wanted to play. She guessed she'd never get to the bottom of what really happened when Grace was living at the cottage without offending Barbara, so she best mind her own business.

Jennifer was saying, "I do love living in the cottage. I'm sorry I never got to meet your husband, Barbara."

Barbara said far too casually, "Oh, I suspect he'll be back, and you'll get your chance."

"Where is he, anyway?" Susan asked.

"Hank is in Rhode Island. He's helping his brother, who has this McMansion renovation project."

"It's the optional. Jen, what do you have?" Susan tapped a tile on the card table. "I thought he was in advertising. What is he doing working construction?"

"It's complicated. How many Jennifer? I can give you two."

Jennifer jerked her head and stared blankly at her rack. "Oh, maybe one. No, two." She was ready to weep. "I'm not sure."

"Can you just pass me something? Anything? Please." Barbara was unhappy with the way the game was going. Too many interruptions, too many mistakes.

Susan felt a vibration from her cell. He'd called once at lunchtime and then after dinner, but she was letting his calls go to voicemail. She expected Gary would try to see her again after the last time. But she was not going to give in. She would ghost him, block his calls. What was the point of continuing their relationship? There was nothing to discuss. Let Gary Rheingold search for the perfect woman. She was done with men. *Done, done, done.*

Barbara's voice was tight. "Jen, are you ready to discard? You were East, remember. When you are East, you discard a tile to begin the game." She looked helplessly at Roseann who just shrugged her shoulders as if to say, 'I'm doing the best I can.'

"Sorry." Jen discarded a three Dot. Roseann patted her on the hand. "Good girl."

The game turned out to be a Wall game. The women began turning over the tiles, the clicking and clacking, the mosaic of colors, suddenly interrupted by a pounding at the front door.

"Who could that be?" For a minute Barbara thought it might be Hank returning, all apologetic, saying he could not stay away. But Hank was in Rhode Island, and they'd agreed a temporary separation was what they both needed. Hank was depressed. He resented her; she was making life intolerable for him, he'd said. All the demands that he change . . . go to this AA meeting, see this therapist she heard about. As for Barbara, she was disgusted with his drinking and drugging. He was better off with his brother Barry, who could handle him. Barbara had no idea how long they would be apart, but truthfully, she was glad he was away. She didn't trust Hank, especially with the new young, attractive tenant. She didn't relish a repeat of whatever he had tried with Grace. Grace was too discreet to talk openly about what had occurred the day she'd gone over to talk to Hank and found them in a clutch. Barbara wasn't born yesterday, and she knew her husband.

The pounding continued. Barbara got up. When she opened the door, Al charged in.

"Now, I want you to stay calm," he said, anything but calm by the tenor of his voice. "I'm sure everything will be okay, but we all have to stay calm. Roseann . . . I need you to stay calm."

The rest of the women turned to Roseann. Her face paled. She got up hastily and stumbled against the card table. "What . . . what is it?"

"Eric and Cindy are back with a court custody order. They were looking for you."

"Oh, my God," Marlene cried.

"The judge ordered in their favor. They are the rightful parents and have a right to be with their son. Social services will have a caseworker checking up on them. But they are taking William back to Florida to be with them."

"Al," Marlene cried. "What should she do?"

"I hate to say this," Susan interjected, suddenly having a change of heart toward William's situation. Roseann was still having a hard time caring for the boy the way they'd all hoped. "Eric and Cindy are his parents and no matter what you think about th—"

"Don't let them take him away. Roseann, talk to your lawyer." Marlene's heart was pounding. This couldn't be happening, she told herself. She put her arms around Roseann and held her close.

"It's no use. I can't win," Roseann's sobs muffled against her chest.

Roseann had hired a lawyer, hoping he could convince the court to make her William's guardian. The lawyer was happy to take her case, but he explained that the judge would be inclined to side with the parents. The parents had stated their case. They were apologetic. Everyone makes mistakes, they pleaded. It was true that Eric and Cindy had abandoned William, but he was their child. They were showing good faith. Eric had gone back to rehab and Cindy had turned up, contrite, begging for forgiveness for running out on both her husband and child.

"If you have any concerns about them, if you think they will harm William, you need to talk to social services and ask them to reevaluate the situation," the lawyer suggested. "But you can't arbitrarily deny his parents their rights to their son unless there is evidence of abuse. There must be proof they are unfit, and there is no evidence other than temporary neglect. They did leave him in good hands with his grandmother while they were away."

"They can't mean to take him from her. Cindy and Eric broke the poor child's heart," Susan moaned. "And now they are breaking hers."

Roseann was rocking back and forth on her feet. "I never had a chance. I am old and sick."

"But you're the best person to take care of William. We should find another lawyer to plead your case," Barbara offered.

"I'm afraid you would be wasting your money and, in the end, not helping William." Al hated saying this, but he knew it was true. He had witnessed cases where children were released to the worst kind of animals—parents who had no right to call themselves parents.

Barbara grimaced.

"I don't know the child, but do you know what William wants?" Jen asked.

"Of course we know what William wants," Marlene cried. "He wants to stay with Roseann."

Roseann pushed away from Marlene. Her voice was steadier now. "That's not true. William wants to be with Cindy. He has been missing his mother the whole time. The poor child needs his mother."

"This is going to be hard, very, very hard, I know. You need to be strong, Roseann. You had better pick the boy up and bring him back home." William had been staying with Marlene and Al since Eric and Cindy had threatened to take him away.

"Roseann, Barbara will drive you home. Barbara, will you stay with her?"

"Sure."

"Al and I will join you after we've talked to William. We have to prepare William for going back with his parents."

Roseann knew this would happen. It was her worst nightmare. She tried to find a reason to forgive the parents. Eric and Cindy's lawyer would make a good case. She reviewed the facts even though they went against her. Eric had gone to rehab. Cindy had gone to Boulder to make a fresh start for herself and her son. And now, she'd returned, trying to reunite with her husband, the boy's father, in a final attempt to keep the three of them together. Cindy would thank Roseann, who had been a big help, but Roseann was not William's mother. Cindy had every right to take William back. What right did Roseann have?

If the courts had ruled in favor of the parents over the grandmother, they surely were considering her condition—old, sick. What was in the best interests of their child?

She hated to admit it, but maybe this was all for the best. The worst was over. Roseann had to think positively. She prayed things would work out in the end. She wasn't going to fall apart. She had her friends, her mah jongg group, to support her. They were there for her, they always were.

CHAPTER TWENTY-FOUR

Barbara had offered to host what would be the group's last Tuesday's mah jongg game. Now that she and Hank were separated, and Hank was in Rhode Island, she had a new perspective on life. She was glad to hand Hank over to his brother, who would, hopefully, straighten him out. She wasn't sure how long he'd be gone, and she wasn't quite sure she wanted him back. Maybe one day, but not yet. He would have to prove himself to her first. And she had other plans for herself although she hadn't sorted them out yet. She was confused.

Barbara was not sure how she felt about being newly single, except she felt safer. She didn't miss the explosive tantrums, the curses, the insults, the meanness, the lies, and the implorations for forgiveness when Hank was sober. A part of her missed the abuse as much as the tenderness. Strangely, the ugly parts of their marriage, she believed, had been the glue that kept them together. She missed her husband. It was hard to let go of someone you loved and to face the future of loneliness.

She had finally admitted to the mah jongg group that she and Hank had separated. "It's a temporary separation." The women read between the lines. They did not say but suspected his leaving had something to do with Grace and her decision to move. Hank was a known womanizer. Susan, her ear to the ground, knew that for a fact.

Today, a pall was cast over the game. So many problems.

Roseann was trying to work through her pain of missing William.

She had become their mah jongg emeritus and had been given the job of coaching Jennifer, who continued to play in their game, even if unenthusiastically

Marlene was East. Disgruntled, she looked at her tiles. What was she going to do with this mess?

Barbara folded her lips. Her thirteen tiles were arranged in suits, but she was unable to detect a pattern.

Marlene crossed over her three tiles to Jennifer who looked at Roseann for help. Roseann pointed to a possible pattern on the card.

"What does C mean?" Jennifer whispered.

"The C is the symbol for a concealed hand, sweetie. Remember, you cannot call a tile for a concealed hand," Susan said dourly. "I suggest you stick with something other than concealed. Unless you have most of the tiles, you are better off with a hand where you can call. Roseann, I thought you were coaching Jennifer."

"I am," Roseann said, unwilling to admit Jen was hopeless.

"Well then, why in heaven's name would you have her do a concealed hand?"

"Ladies, ladies." Marlene reminded the women that they were here to play, not to squabble over who said or did what. "Jennifer is trying her best. Shall we just get on with it? And Roseann, you are doing a fine job. Jen, find a hand and stick with it."

"Too many cooks," muttered Barbara.

Jen was uncomfortable sitting in Grace's seat. She had barely met the woman, but she knew how much the group admired her, and she felt her aura. She stepped out of her high tops and wiggled her toes while she tried to figure out what to do with the tiles that did not look like any pattern on the card. The card was Greek to her, all the letters, numbers, and colors that were supposed to make up a hand but never did. And Roseann was no help. She said it was time Jen figured out what to do on her own.

She had never wanted to play this damn mah jongg. She longed to quit. The truth was she only stayed in the game because she didn't want to risk insulting her new landlord. She had better things to do with her time, like do her laundry and study for next week's quiz.

Barbara had cornered Jen the way she had Grace as soon as she was settled. "We meet on Tuesdays. The next game is at my house. Why don't you stop by and meet the other players?" Only it worked out having Grace (until it didn't).

She had called Susan, Roseann, and Marlene with the good news. "My new tenant is very interested in learning to play, and I thought she could join us on Tuesday. Is that okay?"

They immediately agreed not knowing what they were in for. Things had certainly changed since the beginning of their Tuesday's mah jongg game.

Susan was back working for Dr. Malcolm, who was in the middle of a divorce—or so he claimed.

"I'm planning to move in with him as soon as his divorce is finalized. We're looking for an apartment on the Upper West Side," she boasted. "I always wanted to live in Manhattan, and now it's a dream come true. I just love the restaurants in that part of the city and going to all the shows. Malcolm, I discovered, is a true theater buff. His ex hated Manhattan." Susan threw her head back, inhaling a magical ether. "It is too, too exciting. I don't know how long I will be able to continue playing our Tuesday game once I am living in the city."

Even if being married to Dr. Eliot Malcolm was not exciting, Susan had another chance at romance. Marriage, when she added up the plus and minus columns, meant not having to surf the dating websites and deal with the Gary Rheingolds of the world, and it also meant using Dr. Malcolm's credit card.

As for Marlene and Al, they were planning on taking that cruise for which her father had gotten credit from the cruise line when he explained that his wife had died and that he'd had a heart attack soon after—a white lie. She had written the letter, but her father never sent it. He had come to his senses and given up on the woman Betty who'd made it clear, she never wanted to see him again. Now he was chatting with women his age on a dating website for seniors. He asked Marlene to write his profile, and she'd agreed, but insisted he use a photo that wasn't fifteen years old.

When Al finally got around to telling Marlene he'd invested in some pyramid scheme and lost most of their savings, Marlene didn't tell him she'd known all along what he'd done. She had become suspicious when she saw the envelopes on the hallway table. Every week, there was another notice. She knew something was up from the way Al looked when he found them waiting for him. Marlene had steamed each one open and resealed it, secretly keeping track of their losses. Rather than confront Al, she called their accountant and asked him to research the company.

Barney Hooper, a long-time friend, had advised her to contact the Securities and Exchange Commission, who investigated the pyramid scheme. In the end, Marlene had been able to recoup most of what Al lost. She never told him about the refund she'd received. Instead, she had opened a bank account in her name, where she deposited the money for safekeeping. It was important, she told herself, for a woman to assure her financial independence. *I am no shrinking violet*, Marlene wanted to tell Susan.

When Al had suggested they take that cruise, Marlene balked at the idea. "It's like dancing on my mother's bones. Dad never planned on taking my mom on that trip. Knowing that, how could I enjoy myself?"

"The cruise company doesn't know or care about your father's motives. They just want you to drink as much as you can to drive up the bar bill. There's food all day long. As much dessert as you can eat. Espresso bars. And I heard the midnight buffet is amazing. Besides, your mom had no idea what your father had in mind, so you're not disrespecting her memory if we go. We could use a bit of relaxing after what we've been through."

"I suppose."

"And it doesn't make any sense to let the trip go to waste."

"I suppose."

Since Marlene and Al hadn't been on a vacation in years, and with their daughter having an unplanned grandchild—or so she said, although Marlene suspected she was hoping this one would harness in her husband—Marlene reasoned it was better to go now than wait, when their time would be taken up babysitting the new infant. Marlene was bursting to tell the mah jongg players her news—that they were not only going to be grandparents again, but that they were going on a cruise. Marlene didn't tell Al, but she planned to upgrade their accommodations. They would have a balcony where they could sit and look out at the ocean while having their breakfast and evening cocktails. She told Al it was the cruise line's way of making up for her father having to cancel the trip because of illness. It was another white lie that Al never questioned. And she had the means to pay for the upgrade.

"I think my mom would approve."

"Definitely," Susan said.

"Absolutely," Roseann concurred, trying her best to sound positive. But with William gone, she was facing some tough decisions. She decided against selling her house and possibly moving full time to Florida. Roseann knew she couldn't count on Eric and Cindy staying married and providing a home for William. It was best for William if he had a backup grandmother. Roseann was her grandson's safety net, even if it could only be for ninety-one days at a time. Her plan was to get a seat on the condo board and change some rules.

1. Kids should be allowed to stay with their grandparents indefinitely.
2. Kids should be allowed to use flippers and water wings in the pool.
3. Kids should be allowed to bring their pets when they visited their grandparents.

William now had a puppy he couldn't part with. It was certainly preferable to a hamster!

As for their newest player, Jennifer finally took the plunge and admitted she was just not interested in playing mah jongg. Barbara wasn't disappointed since Jen was a liability to the game anyway.

"I think maybe you women should play bridge or canasta," Jen suggested.

"We'll consider it, but I wouldn't count on it, Jen," Barbara replied. "Mah jongg is in our DNA."

Time passes. There are changes. It looked like the Tuesday mah jongg group might be ready to disband after so many years of being together. Marlene's time would be taken up with her newest grandchild, Susan was moving to New York, Barbara was moving to another state, maybe Colorado, where she would have to get another real estate license. Roseann was going to spend more time in Florida, hopefully with her son, daughter-in-law and grandson. She would still be playing mah jongg, but it wouldn't be the same game her group played in Connecticut. She remembered that there were different mah jongg rules all over the country, but she could adjust.

Of course, there was always virtual mah jongg. They'd all downloaded the app, hoping that way the group could stay together, but it just wasn't the same as playing in person. One by one, the Tuesday women dropped out although they still remained friends.

That last time they met to play at Marlene's, Susan, Barbara, and Roseann returned the Bakelite racks to their compartment and carefully set each tile face down to preserve the Chinese embossing. Her mother's set, in the worn leather case, would reside on the top shelf in Marlene's hall closet until the next generation—possibly her daughter and her friends—decided to take up the game, when each woman would share her own story. Like life, the patterns on the National Mah Jongg League's cards would change through the years, but never the bonds that the game wrought in the players' hearts and minds.

ACKNOWLEDGMENTS

Thank you to Edythe Steffens for harboring me during COVID, where I began writing this mah jongg novel. I am also grateful for the support and skill of my editor Beverley Ehrman, and to all the friends who encouraged me to complete this labor of love.

www.ingramcontent.com/pod-product-compliance
Lightning Source LLC
LaVergne TN
LVHW041939070526
838199LV00051BA/2839